"WHAT DO YOU SAY, MS. BROOKS? DO WE HAVE A deal?"

"Let me get this straight," she managed, "You want me to sleep with you in exchange for the diamond?"

"Just so you do get it straight," Drake responded smoothly, "I doubt there'll be any *sleeping* involved."

Emery felt the flush migrating quickly from her face to the rest of her body, until every tender extremity was softly, vibrantly tingling. No, she definitely wasn't imagining this. "You're joking, right?"

"I promise you, I'm perfectly serious. I can have a contract drawn up, if you'd prefer written proof. It would probably make some fascinating reading, but my attorney's extremely discreet."

A *contract?* Her face went hot with indignant curiosity. She could only imagine what the terms would be.

But of course, she wouldn't even consider signing such a document.

Would she?

Unfortunately, Drake didn't seem willing to wait around to hear her response.

"No answer yet, Em?" he asked, lowering his mouth to her throat, tasting her there, lathing the surface of her skin in slow, melting strokes, taking her a little at a time. "Maybe you'd prefer some physical proof. Maybe I should show you exactly how serious I am."

WHAT ARE *LOVESWEPT* ROMANCES?

They are stories of true romance and touching emotion. We believe those two very important ingredients are constants in our highly sensual and very believable stories in the LOVE-SWEPT line. Our goal is to give you, the reader, stories of consistently high quality that may sometimes make you laugh, sometimes make you cry, but are always fresh and creative and contain many delightful surprises within their pages.

Most romance fans read an enormous number of books. Those they truly love, they keep. Others may be traded with friends and soon forgotten. We hope that each LOVESWEPT romance will be a treasure—a "keeper." We will always try to publish

LOVE STORIES YOU'LL NEVER FORGET
BY AUTHORS YOU'LL ALWAYS REMEMBER

The Editors

Loveswept ® *841*

FLAWLESS

CYNTHIA POWELL

BANTAM BOOKS
NEW YORK · TORONTO · LONDON · SYDNEY · AUCKLAND

FLAWLESS

A Bantam Book / June 1997

ISBN 0-553-44588-X

Published simultaneously in the United States and Canada

Bantam Books are published by Bantam Books, a division of Bantam
Doubleday Dell Publishing Group, Inc. Its trademark, consisting of the
words "Bantam Books" and the portrayal of a rooster, is Registered in U.S.
Patent and Trademark Office and in other countries. Marca Registrada.
Bantam Books, 1540 Broadway, New York, New York 10036.

PRINTED IN THE UNITED STATES OF AMERICA

OPM   10 9 8 7 6 5 4 3 2 1

AUTHOR'S NOTE

Anniversaries are special. When I think of Loveswept celebrating their fourteenth (congratulations!), it reminds me of several events taking place in my own life this year.

My husband and I will be marking our twelfth wedding anniversary in November, but it still feels as if we're on our honeymoon. I can't get over the fact it's been a dozen years, every one of them wonderful, since the day we said "I do." Does that sound hopelessly romantic? I guess I am. But I don't simply write love stories with happy endings, I believe in them from the bottom of my heart.

I wish for every reader out there, the same sweet thrill my heroines have when falling in love, and *staying* in love, forever. I wish for you a hero as sexy, sharp, compassionate, fun, and perfectly romantic as the men I write about, a man as truly heroic as my own husband. Don't ever believe it if someone tells you love and passion fade with time. They don't. They just get better. My marriage is living proof.

This July, my mom and dad will be celebrating their *fiftieth* anniversary. Fifty years! That's pretty impressive evidence for the power of commitment. Their union produced four children (I'm the youngest), ten grandchildren (so far), and who knows how many precocious progeny to follow in the future.

I predict Loveswept will still be going strong in the future. How about a one-hundredth anniversary? Hold on to this book, dear reader. By then it could be a classic!

ONE

Drake Tallen rolled the cool green stone between his fingertips, testing its weight. Twenty carats, minimum, he'd estimate. By far the largest diamond he'd ever found on his land.

And it was *green*.

How appropriate, he thought. A green diamond. The color of sweet, ripe summer in southern Indiana. The cool, compelling color of money.

Not that Drake cared much what the gem's cash value was. He bent down and rinsed it in the bubbling water of Indian Creek, then held it up to the morning sun and let out a low whistle. God, but it was gorgeous.

The shape was intact, a perfect octahedron, the pyramid facets faintly sugar-frosted, but still sharp after a few million years of wear. The edges caught light, flashing shafts of colors in a dazzling visual display. But the greatest beauty lay within, behind the waterdrop windows where the deep earth forces had squeezed carbon into crystalline magic. Where the color was soft and mysterious, as seductive as a woman with her best secrets half-hidden, tempting a man to take a closer look.

No flaws were visible, even to Drake's experienced eye. This was one rare rock. He'd been hunting the streams of Brown and Morgan counties ever since he was a kid and never seen anything like it. It had to be worth a fortune.

Drake considered tossing the stone right back in the creek where he'd found it. He didn't need a fortune. He'd already made one with his own blood, sweat, and soul.

The limestone quarry was finally his after years of gut-wrenching labor. With a rock pick in one hand and a jackhammer in the other, eating dust had been his legacy as far back as he could remember. Dirt, muck, and mud. He'd been up to his elbows in them most of his life. The money had only come later, a by-product that flowed from the business as freely as the perspiration had oozed from his forehead for all those years.

But getting rich had never been his goal.

Proving himself, that's what had mattered. Making something of the wild, willful teenager he'd once been, the backwoods, mixed-breed, unwanted mutt of a boy that no one had believed would ever amount to much. No one except the proud, grizzled old man who'd died, sick and stone broke, barely a decade before. His half-Indian grandfather, who was long gone now, his body reclaimed by the quarry dust that had mercilessly soaked the strength from his life. Gone, but never forgotten.

Drake drew his hand back, dispassionately wondering how many times a flawless octahedron would skip across the surface before it finally hit bottom. But something stopped him from finding out.

The realization that the stone might be worth more to him than mere money. The belief that life's events were never random.

He'd come across this rock for a reason. A reason he doubted had anything to do with luck. No, Drake was the kind of man who preferred to make his own luck. But his grandfather had believed in a universal spiritual order. And in accordance with the ancient tradition of tribal storytellers, through old tales spoken in native tongue, he'd taught Drake to believe in it too.

Fate. Faith. The law of divine reciprocity. Whatever one called it, the power behind that force was still the same. And Drake had his own word for it.

Destiny.

Destiny was the reason this little green gem had wound up in his hand instead of somebody else's. There was no other way to explain it. The diamond had practically been delivered to him on a silver platter. Sent to him from heaven or hell, he wasn't sure which. But either way, it was a talisman he'd been meant to have. And he definitely intended to use it.

The insight came in a flash as he raised the stone

to the light again and stared into its icy interior. The trick was to see it in a different light. To see it not as a diamond, but as a sign of what it could become.

A weapon, for instance, cold, hard-edged, and lethal. Or an ultra-precise tool, tough, practical, and useful. Or simply as a small scrap of bait.

Yes, *bait*, that's what it was.

Drake's hand fisted hard around the small green object. In his mind, it was no longer a diamond, but a costly chunk of green cheese. A lure for his trap. And as such, it was far more valuable. Priceless, in fact. Because it just might be enough to bring *her* scurrying home.

It wasn't fate, Emery Brooks decided. It was simply a cruel, uncanny coincidence that the diamond find of the decade had occurred so close to her hometown. And that Drake Tallen, her ex-fiancé, had been the one to discover it.

Uncanny, because they'd searched that area together when they were younger, scouring hopefully through the streams and forests for the gold and diamonds once deposited there by long-ago glaciers. Cruel, because Drake had sent for her to grade and evaluate the stone, and Nashville, Indiana, was the last place on earth she wanted to be.

And *he* was the last person she'd ever wanted to see again.

But it was already too late to turn back. Her Chicago apartment was more than six hours behind her, along with her plush, Persian-carpeted corner office, prominently displayed via tall glass interior walls on the main floor of Swank's exclusive jewelry store. No, her upscale Michigan Avenue employer wouldn't appreciate it one bit if she decided to ditch this business trip and return home without even looking at the rare green rock. As the company gemologist and gemstone expert, this kind of consulting work was simply part of her job. A typical "house call."

With some very extenuating circumstances.

Least of which was the fact that her greedy boss, Ms. Mia Swank, wanted her to do more than merely gauge the quality of the stone and deliver an opinion to the client. She wanted her to *buy* it. And now that seeing Drake again was inevitable, Emery intended to do far more than give him her professional opinion. She planned to give him a piece of her mind. She planned to return with that diamond, *his* diamond, at any price.

Not that Mia, or her successful chain of Midwest stores, actually needed another diamond, no matter how rare, exquisite, or simply spectacular it was. No matter what wild, mysterious stories were already circulating about it throughout the industry. In fact, the notoriety surrounding the stone was most likely the reason Mia wanted it at all. Simply owning the rock that was said to have the strangest, most sinister curse on it since the infamous blue Hope Diamond was sure to make her the center of attention.

And attention was the one thing Mia loved even more than money.

Swank's, on the other hand, could easily do without the unusual gemstone. Emery knew, perhaps better than anyone, that the luxurious group of stores was knee-deep in diamonds already. Their coffers overflowed with them. Diamonds, emeralds, rubies, and almost every other kind of expensive gem she could name.

But conspicuous consumption and excess inventory were part of what the ritzy chain stood for. Buying the best, and plenty of it, was what kept them in business and kept their wealthy clientele coming back. And kept Emery happily employed.

After five years on the job, she still loved the challenge of it, the excitement of the search for beautiful things. Emery had been drawn to beauty all her life, maybe because she had never been beautiful herself. At least, she'd never felt that way.

Plowed-under cornfields and ripening green pumpkin patches rushed past the wide-open windows of her rental car. Rolling, rural countryside soon gave way to higher hills and roadside apple-cider stands, drawing her deeper into the sun-dappled seclusion of the once-familiar forests. The leaves whispered softly in the late September sky, dry and restless and ready to fall with the first October winds. Emery felt the new season stirring all around her, sensed the cool storms of autumn brewing in the warm afternoon air.

The change was coming soon.

She took a sharp right turn, according to the directions she'd been given, and drove the last few miles down a narrow dirt road. The dusty path finally petered out, dumping her at the base of a strange, secret valley. A vast, sloping field stretched suddenly before her, hidden from above by the high limestone ridges all around.

This had to be the place.

She put the car in park and cautiously stepped outside, somewhat relieved as soon as she'd located the agreed-upon landmarks. There was the metal surveyor's pipe marking the southeast corner of Drake's land. There was the large corral in the distance, with several sleek Arabian-looking horses grazing in the pasture beyond.

She scanned the horizon again, searching but not finding any sign of the house she'd been expecting.

Then she saw him. He was walking toward her from the farthest limestone ridge, tall, tan, darkly silhouetted against the afternoon sky. His hair was black and windblown, his features sculpted in shadow, his eyes focused forward. Focused on her.

Emery drew in a deep breath. Ten years, she thought silently. It was a long time to stay away. But it still wasn't long enough.

Not when just a single glance could bring all the memories rushing back so easily. For a second she felt the air catch in her chest, as if the wind had been knocked right out of her. But she willed herself to keep breathing, forced herself to face the one person she'd tried for so long to forget.

Drake Tallen. The man she couldn't help remembering. The ex-lover she'd left standing at the altar nearly ten years before.

He drew nearer and Emery realized he wasn't entirely alone. Several dogs were following close behind him, four—no, three, herding protectively at his heels in an organized, obedient pack. The largest one, a huge animal that looked to be half wolf, pricked his ears forward and growled a warning at her as they approached.

Drake shushed him with a stare, stopped just a few feet away, and turned toward her. "Emery," he said, speaking her name in that same smooth, hypnotic voice he'd always used to address her. "Welcome home."

Welcome? Emery wondered if he meant it. She wondered why he'd wanted her here at all. There were other experts he might've called, plenty of perfectly competent professionals who would've been all too happy to give him an opinion on the diamond. Professionals he didn't share a past with. It was more than coincidence, she realized, that the man who had once driven her away from her beloved hometown was the same one who'd brought her back to it now.

"Drake," she responded, amazed at how calm her voice sounded, how detached and businesslike, since all of her hard-won, grown-up confidence had suddenly crumbled. The moment she'd seen him again. "It's been a long time."

In Chicago, it had seemed like forever. But here,

now, it felt more like yesterday that she'd fled from him, grasping the skirt of her bridal gown with both hands as she'd run down the aisle and out the door of the church. She could remember it all, every humiliating moment in exquisite, excruciating detail.

The hot tears streaming down her face, the preacher's astounded expression the moment she'd said "I can't" instead of "I do." The sudden gasps of shock in the pews behind her.

The horrifying sight of Drake's normally tan skin as all trace of color quickly drained from his face. A face that had gone white with fury. A face she hadn't laid eyes on since that sickening, life-shattering day.

Until now.

He was far more handsome than she remembered, with a hard-edged elegance about him that had never been there before. His features were stronger now, more darkly defined, as flawlessly cut as the profile on a cold, obsidian cameo. Even his eyes had grayed to a deep icy green, grown wiser, much less wild, beneath the arching, upswept eyebrows.

Only his hair had stayed the same smoldering black, dark and iridescent against the afternoon sky, smooth and sleek as a raven's wing in flight. But it was the set of his mouth that disturbed her the most. The sensual, almost imperceptible curve at the corners silently reminded her of how much pleasure he'd brought her with that mouth. And how much pain she'd suffered in return.

God, but it wasn't fair of him to look *better* than before. Leaner, taller, more essentially male than the younger man she'd run away from. The man who had never really been hers.

Because her older sister was the one he'd been in love with all along.

Tasha, whose eyes were the color of new-laid robin's eggs, her hair as soft and shiny as corn silk, her face a perfect oval. She was the woman Drake had wanted for his wife. Tasha, her drop-dead-gorgeous sister, not her.

The wolf-dog growled at her again, baring his teeth as though he intended to make canine crunchies out of her. As if she were a highly suspicious threat to his master, instead of the other way around.

"Down, Rough," Drake told the creature firmly. "Settle."

As if by magic, the entire doggie three-pack dropped to the ground in an orderly pile of fur and paws and jaws. Emery still felt several sets of eyes staring at her warily, but it was obvious who was in control now. The head dog. The tall, two-legged one whose expression was the most challenging of all.

"I wasn't sure you'd show up," Drake told her, his eyes scanning her thoroughly, with the possessive, very personal curiosity of a former lover. As though it was his right to remember every private, intimate part of her.

Emery bristled. She hated being stared at like

that, and by this man most of all. Was it simple scrutiny she read in his face, or something else? Interest, approval? She promised herself it didn't make any difference. She swore she didn't care what Drake Tallen thought of her one way or the other.

"I'm anxious to see the stone," she explained, carefully reminding herself of the rational, very sane reason for this meeting. To do her job to the best of her ability and fulfill her commitment to Swank's. To buy that diamond from Drake, come hell or high water. And to prove that he wasn't the only one who'd grown wiser over the years.

"Naturally," Drake said. "And I can hardly wait to show you."

Emery didn't miss the tension behind his words, the anticipation that still stretched between them, invisible as air, yet strong and taut as spider's silk. Maybe the straightforward businesslike meeting she'd hoped for wasn't going to be so simple to follow through with. But then, nothing had ever been simple between them before.

Drake Tallen had complicated her life from the beginning. He'd always had a kind of fascinating beauty about him that had frightened and attracted her from the start. A dark, mysterious, masculine kind of beauty. And Emery had always been drawn to beautiful things. Even during that unforgettable summer when she'd been barely fourteen. That summer she'd first noticed him.

She'd watched him in the quarry, cutting limestone, his muscles sleek and suntanned, slick with perspiration. Just the sight of his muddy, sweat-streaked body had made her insides ache. And that one long look had been the start of a terrible teen-age crush.

Before, he'd just been another name on the list of poor, lovesick suckers that Tasha liked to string along. Before, he'd been a roughneck, irresponsible bad boy, with too much rebellion in his veins and too little use for rules or restrictions or authority to suit her very selective older sister. But when the seventeen-year-old Tasha had already broken the heart of every local high-school boy, and Drake had come home that first summer from college, determined to better himself for her sake, she'd finally agreed to date him.

But while Tasha had been Drake's first love, he had been little more than fresh game as far as she was concerned. She had made him wonder and wait, toying with him, testing her considerable feminine powers. Emery, watching it all from the sidelines, had wanted to protect him from her sister's wiles, but she hadn't known how. She'd befriended him instead, become an amusing pest, tagging along behind him everywhere, content to simply be by his side.

Until the summer she'd turned seventeen. The summer Tasha finally broke Drake's heart by secretly marrying another man. Drake was five years older than Emery, a full-grown man of twenty-two. He'd been spurned, hurt, in need of comfort. And

Emery had been more than willing to give it. She'd been eager.

She'd kissed him, begged him to kiss her back. The contact between them had been slow, exploratory, electric. Neither one had expected the kind of charged attraction that flared between them.

"We can't do this, Em. You're just a kid."

"I'm *not*. Kiss me again."

At her urging, her pleading, he'd done more than kiss her. He'd made love to her. Down by Indian Creek, on a starlit summer night, he'd shown her that she wasn't so unattractive after all. He'd proven it to her in that single night of unrelenting passion. And in the morning, she'd awoken in his arms.

With her father standing over them.

"What the hell is going on here?" her dad had demanded.

Emery had wanted to die of embarrassment. Drake had done his best to explain. An hour later he'd agreed to marry her.

Looking up at him now, she knew it was best she'd never gone through with it. It had been hard enough to give him up back then, but it would've been harder still to live her entire life in the shadow of his love for Tasha. Drake Tallen had never been good enough for her older sister, but he'd always been too good for her.

"I'll be staying at Tasha's while I'm here," she explained softly, wondering how he'd react to having the old wound opened again. But if there was any hint of pain or longing left inside him for his past love, he gave no sign of it. Tasha had sworn that any trace of their attraction had long since vanished, but Emery only began to believe it now. So, he was finally over Tasha, she realized. So what? Emery was just as much over him.

Wasn't she?

She kept talking, calmly, coherently, just to prove that she could. To prove to him that she was different now, tougher, stronger than that awkward, heartsick girl who used to hang on his every word. "I guess you know she and Milton bought the house when my folks retired to Florida. We can always meet there later, if you'd like. Why don't you call me, let me know a convenient time?"

Convenient? Drake wasn't sure there would ever be an easy time or place to meet with Emery Brooks again. Seeing her now, after all these years, wasn't exactly the way he'd imagined it. He'd brought her back to put some closure on their past, to get over what had been eating him up for so long. But he felt as if he'd torn something open inside himself instead.

Being dumped by Tasha had been bad enough, but having her little sister leave him standing at the altar when he hadn't even wanted to marry her was worse. Far worse.

He'd taken her to bed in a moment of weakness. And in the morning he'd felt the greatest sense of shame a man could imagine for the dastardly thing he'd done—stealing the innocence of a sweet, sensual girl he didn't love. But he'd been willing to make it up to her and do the honorable thing. He'd been ready to marry her.

And how had she repaid him for it? By bolting in the middle of the ceremony.

Drake knew he should've been relieved. He should've gone down on both knees and thanked his lucky stars for deliverance from a marriage no one had believed in, least of all himself. But he hadn't been happy about it. He'd been humiliated in front of half the town, hurt by the first Brooks sister, scorned by the second.

He'd been angry.

She'd mailed his ring back three days later, apparently too afraid to face him. He'd meant to make her face him now. He found himself confronting his own reaction instead.

The sharp, painful thud in the pit of his stomach, the tight wrench of memory that was twisting far below his gut. A memory of her, cradled in his arms, flat on her back beneath him, with a look of total trust in her warm brown eyes, her hair spilling against the ground in a mass of wild, earth-colored waves. He put his hand out to touch her hair now, just to prove to himself that he could. To prove that the sight of it really hadn't hit him so hard.

"It's funny, Em," he murmured, barely resting his fingers against the pale, neatly pinned tresses, "but I think I've missed you."

The color of it was the same, he thought, still almost blonde in the fading daylight, still shimmering with gold and copper highlights. They were hot, familiar shades that had always reminded Drake of fall in the forest, of the light brown earth singed by flaming autumn leaves. He couldn't help wondering when she'd started wearing it like that, all tugged back and pinned up tight so a man couldn't easily reach it. He wanted to tell her that he far preferred to see it down, falling thick and full around her face.

He wanted to know what the devil was wrong with him. Emery had never affected him like this before. But then, he'd never really seen her as a full-grown woman.

Emery. Her father had named her well. She was like the fine alluvial sand that sometimes washed down through the rivers and streams, making men's hearts skip a beat. The dull, metallic emery sand that old miners knew often marked rich pockets of gold. She was as plain and unremarkable as that gold-bearing dirt, yet there was something about her that fascinated him.

Something that compelled him to look twice this time, to wonder if her outward appearance was no more than a hint of the intriguing riches a man might discover if he only took the time to delve deeper. Curiosity tugged at him, tempted him, until he had to find out. What treasures had she been hiding from him for so long?

"You missed me?" She repeated his words with soft incredulity. "Right. No doubt that's why it took you only ten years to bring me back here. Come on,

Tallen. Let's have the truth. Why did you want to see me again?"

He studied her momentarily, then lifted his shoulders in a casual shrug, unwilling to reveal emotions he didn't completely understand himself. "Your expertise, for one thing," he told her. "You always did know your rocks, Em, even when you were sixteen and tagging along behind me on some treasure hunt. I'd heard you were working at Swank's. Sending for you seemed the obvious choice."

"Strange," she said. "I thought I'd be the last person on earth you'd want to see."

"On the contrary," he told her. "I've been looking forward to it."

"Oh."

She held out her hand then, as if the simple, trucelike gesture might somehow make up for all that had happened between them. As if politely shaking hands would compel him to forgive and forget how she'd ditched him as a bridegroom, kicked him when he was down, deserted him.

He ignored the invitation to touch her. Drake didn't want to shake hands, not just yet. He wanted to tighten his fingers around her sweet, feminine throat and slowly, thoroughly strangle her. Why had she run out on him that way? He wanted to know, once and for all. He *needed* to know, finally. This time he wasn't going to let her drop him so easily, without the slightest attempt at an explanation. This time he intended to get some answers.

Involuntarily, he found himself studying her left hand, searching for any sign of a ring. Her third finger was still bare, he realized with a sense of satisfaction. He'd heard she'd never married, but the certainty of it still hit him with something very close to relief. So, she'd never met the right man, had she? Did she ever regret the decision she'd made, not to marry him? he wondered. Or had her fast-track career and her big-city single life been enough to satisfy her?

"What about you, Em?" he asked her. "You didn't have to take this job and yet you still showed up. Any particular reason?"

"Curiosity, I suppose."

"Personal or professional?"

"Maybe a little of both," she confessed. "I wanted to see the diamond, and . . ."

"And?"

"To see how you were doing, how things turned out. We *were* friends once, in case you don't remember. At least I always looked up to you."

"Pestered me, you mean," he corrected her, grinning at the memory of a fiercely determined fifteen-year-old he couldn't seem to shake loose from his heels.

She didn't rise to his teasing the way she might have once, with a smart slap on the arm or a soft, playful punch to his solar plexus. She ignored it, with a gracious, very grown-up aplomb that spun him a hundred and eighty degrees from the stubborn, kinda cute kid he remembered. The woman in front of him was all adult, still stubborn, it seemed, but completely in control of herself.

She waved her arm toward the far horizon, gesturing to the valley around them. "I knew you'd be a success like this, with a big place of your own. Horses. Lots of acreage. You always did love the land. I'm happy for you."

"I've been lucky," he said. "I own the quarry now."

"I know. I passed by it on my way into town. Saw your name on the sign."

Drake wondered if the words were deliberate, since they stung him just as sharply as a full slap on the face. She'd seen his name on the sign. Guess that meant she hadn't made much effort to keep up with him all these years. Hadn't cared enough to ask. Or maybe she just hadn't wanted to know.

"Surprising, isn't it?" he said lightly. "Not exactly the way this town expected me to turn out."

She smiled at him then, sending a fierce jolt of memory shafting through him. Emery had never been drop-dead beautiful, but that smile of hers could still stop a man in his tracks. It was warmer than a shot of home-brewed, eighty-proof cider on a snowy February day. Sweeter than a crisp, sunripe apple, stolen from a forbidden orchard branch by a hungry boy.

"I guess we're both older now," she said, her voice calm and cautious, matter-of-fact. "Both wiser. So maybe we should get this matter taken care of as soon as possible. Get straight down to business. I'm prepared to do more than merely grade and evaluate that diamond you discovered. If we can agree on a fair price, I'd like to purchase it. For Swank's, of course."

Drake would've applauded her for sheer audacity if her words hadn't pricked him quite so sharply. So *that* was why she'd come here, after all. She wanted to negotiate with him, did she? He finally had something she needed.

That wasn't at all the way the scenario had played in the past. Back then, she'd refused even to talk to him. She'd left him and never looked back.

They'd get down to business all right, Drake agreed silently. He'd see to that. If she was lucky, very lucky, she might even get her diamond deal. But it was going to cost her plenty, in the form of some straightforward answers. The truth was what she would have to pay him, *if* he decided to sell. Yes, he planned to make her pay. And in the process, he was going to get her out of his system for good.

"Fine," he told her, "business it is. But it'll have to be here. Tonight. Nine o'clock."

"Nine?" she asked doubtfully. "That's a little late for a meeting, isn't it? I don't much like being out at night."

"Don't you?" he asked skeptically, the corners of his lips tilting into a slow, knowing smile. "From what I remember, Em, you used to like it a lot."

Emery flushed to the tips of her earlobes, realizing he was right. Knowing he still remembered that long-ago evening just as accurately as she did. Every passionate, sensual, damning detail.

The smell of his skin on hers with the night mist all around them and the cool, damp ground beneath. The music of the creek as the water lapped the rocks and the fireflies blinked their secret messages back and forth across the field. The sweet, searing heat of Drake above her, inside her, filling her.

She'd never known a night like that since. Never felt that way for another man. But then, there was only one Drake Tallen.

"You know what I mean," she whispered. "Please don't make this more difficult than it has to be."

"Difficult?" he asked. "I imagine it's hard on you, Em, to have to stick around this time and fight for something you want. But no one's keeping you here against your will. You can still run away. You've always been good at that."

"It *is* hard," she admitted, trying not to let him see how squarely his gibe had hit home. He just didn't understand, she thought bitterly. Drake Tallen had always had what she wanted. Always *been* what she wanted. But she was here for something else this time. And this time she wasn't about to run away.

"You're not the only one who's changed. I'm not seventeen anymore, in case you haven't noticed. And the past is simply that. It doesn't make any difference now."

"Are you sure about that?" He cupped her chin

with his hand, tilting her face up even farther until she had no choice but to stare into those challenging green eyes.

She closed her own eyes briefly, steeling herself against the sensation of his strong, skillful fingertips resting against her face. Those hands had been her undoing back then, touching her in places she couldn't believe, in ways she'd never imagined. He'd brought her to slow, aching ecstasy with them once. Today they reminded her too much of the man she'd been in love with.

The one who raced Indy-bound trains on horseback for his entertainment, who might meditate for an entire hour without moving, or dive, naked, from the dangerous quarry cliffs into the deep, forbidden blue-water pools below. Emery had secretly watched him do that once, her heart in her throat, her mouth dry with terror and amazement. And illicit, unspeakable desire.

She'd been frightened by the feeling, the same one she was experiencing now. She took a small step backward, just out of his reach.

"Look, Drake, I think we'd better get this straight from the start. I'm not here to play games."

"Too bad," he answered, laughing, dropping his hand back down by his side. "That was another thing you were very good at, Em."

"I appreciate you giving me the first shot at the diamond," she went on, ignoring his remark.

"What are old friends for?"

"If it's everything I'm hoping it is—"

"It's better," he assured her. "Too bad we didn't find it together back then, on one of our afternoon rambles. . . ."

Emery lost her train of thought as soon as his voice trailed away. She was caught up in the memories his words had revived, all the lazy summer afternoons they'd spent sluicing for gold flecks in the bubbling country streams.

Drake had taught her how to search for the small placer deposits with nothing but a rusted metal pan and a strong sense of hope. But the buried earth treasures had always eluded them. Instead of growing suddenly rich from their finds, they'd been seduced by the warm sun, the lush, leafy forests, and the sweetness of the hours spent alone together.

"Maybe it would've changed things," he added. "It's harder, isn't it, to walk away from a rich man than a poor one?"

"Not for me," she said flatly. "It wouldn't have changed anything."

"Of course not for you, Em. I was thinking of Tasha, actually. Stability was what she'd wanted all along. Safety, security. I was just too down-in-the-dirt proud and impoverished to provide it. No doubt you would've hightailed it away from me no matter what."

Emery tried to blink back the dull ache behind her eyes, tried to swallow against the lump that had formed at the base of her throat. She *would* have left him, rich or poor, but only because she'd had no other choice. It wasn't exactly fair to ruin a man's entire life just for one night of reckless passion. Especially not since she'd been the one to seduce him.

Not when she'd discovered, five minutes before her wedding ceremony was to begin, that her soon-to-be husband was far from over her stunning older sister.

"No doubt," she agreed calmly, fighting back the unbidden emotions and trying to regain control of the conversation. "But that's all water under the bridge now, isn't it?"

"If you say so."

"What I've been *trying* to say is, if the stone's everything I'm hoping for, I'm prepared to make you a generous bid."

"Of course, Ms. Brooks," he said softly, signaling to the three menacing mongrels at his feet that it was time to take their leave. "Just don't forget to be here at nine," he added as he turned his back on her and began to walk away. "I can hardly wait to hear what you have to offer."

TWO

Drake felt the pulse of the jackhammer pounding through him, the beads of sweat bouncing off his forehead from the raw, blistering vibration, but his grip on the handles never wavered. It grew stronger instead, tightening, tensing along with every other muscle in his body against the jarring jolts. He didn't fight the merciless machine or the pain it inflicted so savagely along the length of his arms and back and torso. He embraced it, melded himself with the electric steel instrument, matching movement with movement, action with reaction until the metal and his mind became one.

The quarry was closed, the workmen long since gone home to their suppers, but he was still there, hammering away at a massive block of limestone, fighting back the demons of the past in the only way he knew how. With his own bare hands and as much hard work as his body could handle.

The ache in his shoulders was strong, the grueling, grinding labor so familiar it brought him a sense of relief. He'd been just fifteen when he'd started busting rubble, struggling to support himself. His parents had split up by then, gone their separate ways, and left him to live with his grandfather.

But the old man had been crippled with arthritis from his own life of hard quarry labor, and the two of them had barely scraped by. Instead of his grandfather looking after Drake, he'd looked after his grandfather. Just watching the old man suffer, struggling proudly against the pain, had made Drake wince. It had made him swear vengeance against mining management for working his granddad nearly to death, then firing him two months short of retirement. Just two months shy of a measly pension that the quarry owners preferred not to pay.

Drake had promised himself he would pay *them* back someday.

And that's exactly what he had done. He'd sweated blood for years, made his way to the top on a mountain of mud, saved every penny they'd tossed him. Biding his time, he had organized a takeover, begged for investors to back him. And in the end, he'd bought them all out.

But battling for control of the quarry had cost him much more than money. Now that it was his, he didn't know how to stop fighting for what he believed in. Or how to let go of the bitterness without working up a heavy sweat. Breaking up rocks was more to him than a simple expense of excess energy.

It was jaw-gritting therapy, a pulverizing, primitive release.

Becoming sole owner of the business had set the scales back in balance, restored some sense of dignity to the old man's memory, but it hadn't set Drake free of the monsters that hounded him. The shame he'd felt was still with him, gnawing at his gut like some guilty secret he'd once been too proud to reveal.

Ignorant town trash, that's all the Tallens had ever been. Drake had heard those words so often when he was younger, he'd believed them. He'd been ashamed of his own heritage, of his parents' breakup, and worse, of his grandfather, who'd grown up during the Depression and lived a hard, humble life. He'd loved the old man like nobody's business, but he'd been too full of pride to bring his friends around the small woodland shack that had been their home.

They'd kept to themselves instead, and Drake had learned the ways of the forest, sought his roots in the traditions of tribal tales and teachings his grandfather passed down to him. The old man had taught him things he'd never heard in school. How to seek his spirit guide. How to live in harmony with the land. How to be a man.

He'd shown him all this through legends and lore, through patience, understanding, and compassion, loving him the way his father should have. And Drake had dishonored him in return.

He stopped to wipe the dust from his safety goggles, then flipped the switch on the hammer up to full speed and let the pebbles fly. And let himself remember what was the hardest of all to admit. He'd resented the legacy of abject poverty the elder Tallen had left him. He'd been embarrassed to be the descendant of a poor, beaten-down old man who'd never seen the inside of a schoolroom or had more than ten dollars to his name.

Patience was the only thing his grandfather had had plenty of, a peaceful willingness to roll with the punches life had thrown at him. His calm acceptance of an unfair fate had frustrated Drake beyond belief. He'd vowed he would never sit idly by and take what circumstances handed him. He'd promised to deliver a few of his own punches at destiny instead.

And when the opportunity had come, he'd hit back hard. He'd bettered himself by working his way through college, beating the odds before they'd had a chance to beat him down. But no matter how hard he pounded the hammer now, no matter how many stones he crushed, the guilt he had suffered for his family shame never went away completely. And he wasn't sure if he could ever forgive himself for it.

Emery stood on the sidewalk outside the Bean Blossom Bridal Shop and hugged her sister hard. "Tasha," she said, pulling back to take a good long glance at her thirty-year-old sibling. "You look incredible," she added honestly, with only a slight pang of envy in her voice.

Tasha actually was breathtaking, even prettier than she'd been ten years earlier when Drake had been in love with her. Not that Emery could blame him for it. What man wouldn't fall for a face and figure as perfect as her sister's? She was so stunning that strangers on the streets of Nashville still stopped and stared when she walked by.

Emery, at twenty-seven, was used to fading into the background by now. Used to being known as the "smart" sister. The only problem with being smart was that you understood what people meant when they said that. What they really meant was that you were nowhere near as nice-looking as your older sister.

Tasha hooked their arms together and led her into the store. "You're holding up pretty well yourself, sis. Sorry I couldn't meet you at the house, but you remember how busy the shop gets this time of year. Four weddings this weekend, the annual autumn ball next Saturday, and every one of my customers wants 'something unique.' I don't know how Mom ever kept up with it all and raised the two of us at the same time!"

Emery looked around the cottage-sized front room, which was even smaller than she remembered, and sighed. She'd never wanted to set foot in this place again, for good reason. There were far too many memories attached to it.

Memories of her mom, let down after Tasha's no-frills elopement to Professor Milton Matthews, throwing herself into Emery's shotgun wedding with enough enthusiasm for ten mothers of the bride. The attention had been overwhelming for a teenager who'd rarely warranted a second look from anyone. There'd been plans, invitations, guest lists, menus, silk flowers enough to choke the church aisles, and so many birdseed baggies they could've fed a flock of pigeons for a month.

Too bad it'd all been wasted.

But no matter how painful Emery's memories were, it was still impossible to enter this tiny fantasy of a bridal boutique and remain unaffected. Here, even the most cynical of feminine hearts was in danger of being swept away and losing every shred of common sense to impossibly romantic daydreams.

Lace and satin, silk and tulle all flowed together in an ethereal, enchanting fairyland of white. Except for the central stand of full-length mirrors and the twinkling spun-glass chandelier suspended from the ceiling, not a single surface was left unembellished. Pearls and roses, swags and ribbons and filmy, see-through netting adorned everything from the simplest suit-dress to the fanciest full-train, formal gown, complete with rhinestone tiara.

"It's super, Tasha," Emery told her. "Looks like you're keeping up the family tradition just fine. And I know Mom's happy about it."

Naturally their mother was ecstatic over Tasha's choice of careers. It had always been Mrs. Brooks's dream to see both of her beautiful daughters marry, then take over the family business, in that specific order. The problem was, only one of her daughters was beautiful. And only one of them had lived up to all her expectations.

Emery, unfortunately, had let her down. The day she'd run away from her own wedding, all those maternal hopes had been crushed. Ruined, right along with the Bean Blossom Bridal Shop's most exquisite bridal gown.

Tasha locked the door behind them and flipped the card in the front window to CLOSED. "Come on into the back," she suggested. "We can chat while I check on the new shipment of evening dresses. They made it just in time."

They threaded a path through the tidy back stockroom where row upon row of gowns lined the neatly packed wall racks. A Victorian love seat with two matching chairs offered much-needed sanctuary for frazzled mothers, energetic maids of honor, and worn-out brides to be.

Tasha made her way to the antique mahogany coffee table, where a floral tea service had been laid out, and poured two steaming cups of a soothing sassafras blend. "Now relax," she said, handing a cup to Emery and settling down beside her on the love seat. "We have so much to catch up on, I don't even know where to start. But first, I'm dying to hear how your meeting went. Did you see Drake? Was he still angry? You've got guts, Em, I'll have to give you that. I don't know how you had the courage to face him again."

Emery gave her sister a slow, rueful smile. "It wasn't easy," she responded, grateful for the sweet refreshing liquid, the calming warmth flowing to her hands through the smooth china cup. "I don't think he was exactly happy to see me, and the feeling was mutual. Anyway, the hardest part's over with. Now that the initial awkwardness is past, we can get down to business. And if I end up buying the diamond for Swank's, it'll all be worth it."

"Your job must mean a lot to you," Tasha said, shaking her head, "if you're willing to go up against Drake Tallen just to get that stone. He's changed, Em. He's still independent, still likes to do things his own way, but he's rich and powerful now, well respected in this town. I hope you know what you're doing."

"I love my work," Emery answered simply. "I'm good at it. But getting this gem for Swank's would be the biggest coup of my career." Not to mention a very satisfying personal success. It would feel good to win that diamond from him. The fact that he was the one who owned it would only make the challenge, and the victory, that much sweeter. "And I knew Drake long before he was a big shot, remember? He doesn't scare me one bit."

It was a lie, of course. Drake Tallen did frighten her. How else could she explain the pounding in her heart, the perspiration on her palms, the weakness in her knees, all of which had started the moment she'd laid eyes on him again? It was either fear, she decided, or something far worse.

Excitement. Desire.

Oh lord, she wasn't still attracted to him was

she? No way. Certainly *not*. At least, she'd rather die than admit it to anyone, most of all herself.

"And I'm not about to let that diamond slip through my fingers without a fight," she added, just for good measure. Just to remind herself how much she meant it. She wasn't going to give up just because the very bad boy she'd once been in love with had since become a VIP.

Especially not since she'd read the mocking challenge in the depths of Drake's angry, adamantine eyes. As much as she hated to admit it, she was stung by what he'd said. Stung by the suggestion that she was likely to run away again. If that's what Mr. Big Man Tallen expected of her now, he was in for a serious surprise.

"I can see you've already made up your mind," Tasha observed in apparent sisterly understanding. "Will you let me know if there's anything I can do to help?"

Emery nodded, grateful for the support. She and Tasha had never been the closest of friends, but maybe this visit would help to change that. At least she could begin to acknowledge that her sister had never intentionally meant to hurt her.

"Thanks," Emery added. "Letting me stay with you and Milton is enough for now. But don't expect me at the house until later. I'm meeting Drake again at nine."

"Tonight?" Tasha asked in mild surprise. "You *are* determined, aren't you?"

Emery nodded calmly. "I have to be. If only to prove to him I'm not the coward he thinks I am."

If only to prove it to herself.

Emery's resolve didn't start to waver until she'd actually set foot on Drake's land again. Everything looked different in the dark, as if a cloak of midnight mist had settled around the shoulders of the valley, enveloping her in its soft, cooling shadows. This time the secluded meeting spot seemed strangely dense and spooky.

And this time he was waiting for her.

As soon as her eyes adjusted to the light, she noticed him. Sitting astride the most magnificent sable stallion she'd ever seen. The sweater and slacks he wore were black enough to pull off a jewel heist and fit the corded contours of his body so closely, they made her think twice about what she was doing there. Drake Tallen was worse than dangerous. He was *devastating.*

He looked so supremely confident staring down at her, Emery knew he'd never doubted that she'd show. Gazing up into those self-assured, unwavering green eyes of his, she began to wonder why she had come back at all. He wasn't the kind of man who'd give up anything without a struggle, least of all a rare green stone he might not want to sell. Least of all to her.

"Leave the car," he told her quietly, "and climb

up in front of me. It's another half mile to my place."

The stallion snorted impatiently, stamping and pawing at the ground as his shoulder muscles rippled in the moonlight. Emery eyed him doubtfully, estimating the distance between the saddle and the safety of the earth. "No, thanks," she shot back. "I can drive. No reason to waste a perfectly good rental car."

"Only one," he responded, easily controlling the restless animal with a single deft tug on the reins. "There's no more road. And unless you've got four-wheel drive on that very useless vehicle, it's not moving another inch. Now, hop up."

Hopping was the last thing Emery had on her mind, just then. Leaving sounded far more appealing. Leaving Drake and the diamond, and the world's tallest, most terrifying stallion, and never looking back. Unfortunately, her pride was even stronger than her fear. And the horse wasn't really what had her so scared.

"Forget it," she told him, crossing her arms in front of her with what she hoped was a convincing show of spirit. "You lead the way and I'll walk."

"You'll *ride*," he insisted, leaning forward and grabbing her under the arms, hoisting her onto the stallion's bare back before she had time to object. "We can argue about it later," he added, the minute she opened her mouth to protest. "Funny, Em, but that's one of the things I miss about you the most. You always did know how to put up a good fight."

"Only because you were so good at picking them," she countered, shaken by the strength and speed with which he'd moved. By the unexpected position in which she suddenly found herself.

No matter what Drake had said about her inclination to argue, Emery's heart just wasn't in it at the moment. She was too busy trying to adjust to the feel of his arms wrapped around her again. To the broadness of his chest pressed full against her back as the horse started its swift canter across the valley. To the rough, rocking contact of Drake's long, wool-clad legs as they inexorably locked with hers.

"Besides," she added, feverishly imagining that small talk might take her mind off the physical reality of the moment, "that's not the part I miss at all."

"Oh?" he asked softly, and Emery felt the word brush faintly against her ear, erotic and teasing as a slow feather stroke. "And what part is that? What do you miss the most?"

She felt her face flushing warm in the darkness and was grateful he couldn't see it. Grateful he couldn't tell how painfully fast her heart was racing.

"I didn't mean it that way," she managed. She wanted to add that she didn't miss *anything* about the past, but she couldn't quite force her mouth to form the words. They were so far from the truth, it seemed a sacrilege to say them. She missed everything about Drake, God help her.

"No, I don't suppose you did," he agreed calmly.

"Well, good for you, Em. No regrets, right? Otherwise, you wouldn't have stayed away so long."

"So long?" she asked bitterly, in spite of her resolve to keep their encounter as calm and professional as possible. He was the only reason she'd stayed away. The only reason it hurt so much to return. "I'd say it hasn't been long enough."

"Clearly not," he agreed, laughing. "Since you still lose your temper with me far too easily."

"My temper," she said angrily, "isn't the only thing I lost too easily with you."

She felt his body go rigid behind her and instantly regretted the words. Her virginity had been a gift she'd given to him freely. The physical love they'd shared was a memory she would always treasure. She'd never been sorry for it. Never, until she'd overheard him talking with Tasha in the vestibule of the church, just moments before her wedding.

The damning words he'd whispered to her older sister had cut through her like a knife.

"I still love you, Tasha," the hidden Emery had heard him say.

"I know," had been her sister's thoughtless response. "I've seen that look before. It's temporary, I promise. You'll get over it."

"*You* should be the one wearing my ring," Drake had answered heatedly. "It isn't much, I know. But I bought it for *you*, Tasha. Long before Professor Matthews ever asked you to elope. Hell, why did you have to go and marry *him* before you even gave me a chance?"

"Get over it," Tasha had told him cruelly. "I don't love you. Emery does."

"Right," he'd shot back bitterly. "At least one of the Brooks sisters wants me. Almost as much as I want you."

Emery hadn't stuck around to hear more. She'd barely been able to pull herself together before the bridal march had started. She'd hardly been able to follow Tasha, her traitorous matron of honor, down the aisle through the haze of tears and hurt, to where Drake was standing, waiting for her.

And wanting someone else.

No, she wasn't sorry if her angry comment just now had hit home. She didn't *want* to hurt Drake. But she doubted anything she could say would compare with those awful whispered words she'd lived with for the last ten years.

He brought the horse to a sudden stop at the edge of the valley, checking their progress beside a steep limestone wall. "I'm sorry you remember it that way," he said softly, and swung himself easily to the ground.

Emery might've been deceived by his casual demeanor if she hadn't noticed his hands. His grip on the bridle seemed gentle enough, but his knuckles were taut and white. She had stung him after all. Well, maybe she was glad of it. Glad to get a response that proved their lovemaking had at least meant *something* to him.

"Get down," he suggested. "And I'll be happy to refresh your memory as to who started what that night."

Emery clutched involuntarily at the stallion's massive jet mane. If Drake wanted her down there with him, he was going to have to peel her off his horse, one reluctant limb at a time.

"I'm not budging," she promised him stubbornly, "until you explain exactly why we've stopped here."

"Worried, pet?" he asked solicitously, wrapping the reins around a nearby fence rail, securing the horse and leaving both of his hands free. "Why? You used to trust me implicitly."

Emery willed herself to ignore the near-forgotten nickname and the mass of conflicting emotions the sound stirred in the pit of her stomach. *Pet.* She couldn't believe she'd ever let him call her that. It was the kind of easy, affectionate label you might give to a favorite dog or cat. Or a tag-along teenage girl whose face was as full of the same unconditional adoration.

"I *used* to follow you around like a puppy. Let's just say I'm not so eager to obey anymore."

"Obey?" he repeated, turning back toward her with a forced smile. "As in love, honor, and obey? Since when were you eager to do any of those things?"

Emery felt herself being dragged bodily from the horse in a movement even faster than the one he'd pulled her up with. And just as swiftly as before, she landed smack dab in the middle of Drake's arms again. Only this time the two of them were face-to-face.

Eye to eye. And almost mouth to mouth.

If it wasn't for the difference in their heights, their lips would already be touching. If it wasn't for those few, final, agonizing inches. Was he going to kiss her now? she wondered. Or was a slow, seductive tease more what he had in mind? She closed her eyes as the anticipation mounted, becoming almost unbearable.

Drake swore softly to himself that he definitely *wasn't* going to do it. In fact, he was so deadly determined *not* to kiss her that the proximity of Em's mouth near his was exquisite, excruciating torture. The heat of her breath, sweet and shaky, mingling with his in the cool night air. The soft, wet part of her lips. God, but how willingly they'd opened for him once, so achingly ripe, so ready to take him in.

He'd felt them part from passion before, felt himself harden with shock-wave response. But his current desire wasn't as simple as it had been back then. He'd needed her that summer. He'd buried his grandfather and lost Tasha's love all in the space of a few short weeks. The ache inside him had been rough, awesome, wrenching. So fierce that when Emery'd come along and offered to soothe it, he hadn't had the strength to resist.

Now he wasn't sure he wanted to resist her. He wanted to punish her for leaving him. To press her hard up against the nearest tree and reclaim what she'd taken away.

He let her go instead. After turning the stallion loose in the corral, he headed straight toward the hillside without bothering to look back.

Emery followed. But she was so busy wondering where they were going that she nearly collided with Drake's broad back when he finally stopped. Outside a tall, narrow opening in the limestone hill where a half-hidden entrance tunneled straight into the hard cliff wall.

"Here we are, Em," he told her. "Home at last."

She looked at the looming black void in the valley wall, trying to decide if it was some sort of trick. Drake didn't *live* here, did he? In a cave? Wasn't that pushing the envelope of individuality just a bit too far? She wouldn't have to go in there with him to see the diamond.

Would she?

He was bluffing her, most likely, toying with her like a sleek, clever tomcat teasing a small brown mouse.

"You're kidding, right?"

His teeth gleamed white in the moonlight and he looked just a little too pleased with himself. A little too pleased with her shocked reaction.

"I never kid," he told her, then ducked and disappeared inside.

Emery felt a wave of disbelief wash over her, followed shortly by a full-blown attack of cold, practical common sense. She *wasn't* going in there. Her determination to score that stone for Swank's was one thing. Following Drake Tallen into a dark, forbidden den was another. Besides, those three dogs were probably lurking somewhere on the other side, guarding the entrance like the hounds of hell, just waiting to pounce on her as soon as she stepped inside.

And what was it the locals had nicknamed that accursed stone again? *The Devil's Diamond*. Named after the dark-haired devil who'd found it, no doubt. And the only way to get it was to accompany Lucifer inside his lair.

"The diamond," he'd say, "in exchange for your soul." But Emery wasn't about to make such a bargain. She'd gambled her heart that way and lost it once, and she had no intention of risking it again, certainly not for the sake of a rock. Satan would just have to pick another sucker this time.

But before she had a chance to turn and leave, the entrance to the cave glowed golden. There was light coming from somewhere within. Warm, welcoming, wonderful electricity. Curious, she took a few steps closer and peered inside.

Drake was leaning patiently against a rough wooden door, calmly observing her. "Chickening out again?"

She took a deep breath, swallowing hard. "Not a chance. I'm just not too fond of small spaces." Or bats or snakes, or any other creepy crawly cave-dwelling creatures. Not to mention tall, dark, and dangerous demons.

"Don't sweat it," he said, apparently taking pity on her and opening the entry door so she could see inside. "The cavern itself is huge." He flipped a light switch on the inside wall. "With all the modern conveniences."

Emery blinked in sudden awe. Drake's living quarters were better than huge. They were beautiful. She crossed the threshold, compelled by the incredible sight.

The light within was soft and sparkling, glistening against the vast calcite ceiling like the dawning sun over night-frozen drifts of snow. Stalactite formations studded the cavern roof, tall as teardrop chandeliers hung from a palace ballroom, dripping with icicle jewels. But the walls were the most amazing of all, gorgeous and glittering and covered with crystals of rich, mysterious purple. Amethyst crystals.

Drake's "house" was more than a simple cave. It was a king-sized geode formed by nature, a subterranean grotto of solid gems.

Emery struggled for words. "It's . . . fantastic."

He followed her in, closing the door behind him. "I thought you'd approve."

She scanned the cavern again slowly, still trying to absorb its stunning glory. It was like a dream she'd had once, as a little girl, of a sparkling palace with a handsome prince to match. Only that castle had been somewhere in the sky instead of ten feet beneath the earth. And she'd never imagined sharing it with the Prince of Darkness.

On second glance, she realized some of the man-made features were as compelling as the natural ones. The floor had been scoured flat more or less, right down to solid bedrock. Plush area rugs divided the different living areas. There was a kitchen of sorts, with appliances of polished steel, a separate den with a wet bar and dining table, and a huge leather couch at the great room's center, mounded with rich velvet pillows.

"Very impressive," she murmured. Actually, it was overwhelming. In a sumptuous, exotic, Ali Baba kind of way. "So you really *do* live underground."

"It suits my purposes."

"Water, electricity, the works, huh?"

He shrugged. "I'm not into roughing it. Not any longer."

Emery had a sudden flashback of the run-down little hut where Drake had lived while looking after his grandfather. A hovel was all it had been, but Emery had felt a secret thrill when he'd let her tag along there. Tasha herself had never been asked inside, probably because she would have lifted her perfect little nose and sniffed at the shabby surroundings. But Emery hadn't minded the lack of luxury one bit. Just being there with him had been enough.

Looking around now at Drake's living quarters reminded her just how much his circumstances had changed. He'd worked his way up from hovel to palace in a pretty short time. And it wasn't hard to guess what had driven him. His need for justice against the previous quarry owners, for the way they'd treated his grandfather.

She was glad he'd won that battle, since the cause had been a good one, but it made her even more wary of his potential wrath. Was he still angry at her, she wondered, for bolting at the ceremony and offering him no explanation? Just how far would he be willing to go to wreak some sweet revenge for what she'd done?

A second glance around the cavern didn't do much to ease the tension that was building inside her. His fantastic home was starting to feel more like a fortress all the time. The kitchen counter was a solid block of granite. The lighting and electronics state-of-the-art. The setting so secure and private that permission from the master was required to enter. There was no other way in.

Or out.

She cast a speculative glance at the door, suddenly wondering if Drake had locked it behind him. Suddenly remembering just how strong a man he was. And what a vulnerable position she'd put herself in.

He let out a soft laugh and spoke as though he'd read her mind. "Maybe I *have* locked you in, pet. Maybe the stone was just an excuse to lure you here, all alone, so I could carry out some dastardly deed."

"Murder, for instance?" she asked sweetly. "Go

ahead," she suggested boldly. "Give me your worst. Do me in."

"You've underestimated me, Ms. Brooks. Doing you in would be too easy. And it would be far from my worst."

"You're right," she admitted. "There's always torture. Maybe you'd like to chain me naked to the wall, force me to—" She stopped in mid-sentence, her face growing hot at the very idea of what she'd been about to say. Of course, she didn't believe Drake had anything of that sort in mind. She'd dreamed it up in her own sick, stress-filled mind. And that was exactly what made it so embarrassing.

"To what, Em?" he asked softly, even though she knew he'd understood. "Oh, yes, *that*. I suppose that *would* be the ultimate torture."

She turned from him, flushing, and headed for the door. Locked, barred, or bolted, she didn't care. She would kick it down if she had to.

But the knob turned easily in her hand.

It had never been locked. Drake had been bluffing. He'd never even considered keeping her there against her will. And somehow that just made it all the more humiliating.

When the door swung open, she didn't stop. She just kept running, straight out into the dark night, straight into the fresh, open air. Straight into a silent swarm of bats.

Bats! They were swooping down on her, streaming from some unseen opening in the valley wall, flocking around her face, her hands, her hair. Emery swore she wouldn't faint. She'd never fainted in her life, not once, and she wasn't about to start now, not while Drake was probably watching. Probably enjoying every moment of her misery.

Hell, *no*, she wouldn't faint.

She would scream and scare the bats right back. She would scream and close her eyes so she wouldn't see them.

Unfortunately, her spur-of-the-moment plan had only one drawback. She couldn't see anything else, either. Couldn't tell where she was running.

Or exactly what she'd run into when she felt the blow to her forehead. Right before the world faded away.

THREE

The first thing Emery noticed when she opened her eyes was a vivid canopy of color overhead. A ceiling of lustrous Persian fabric, shot through with spun gold, in the shape of a soft, cocooning tent. Heaven, she decided, must look something like this. No puffy clouds or pale boring blue, but rich and kaleidoscopic and so infinitely patterned, it would take an eternity to comprehend.

"Am I dead?" she asked out loud, not necessarily expecting an answer. Just hearing her own voice gave her some small sense of comfort. At least it was an encouraging sign. Far too normal and humdrum for the here-ever-after.

The tent curtain parted and she shortly discovered her eyes were in perfect working order as well. Drake stood over her, looming like a phantom from some dark, dreamy underworld, his sensual, shadowed face full of genuine concern.

"You're conscious." His voice was low when he spoke, but the tone was rough and rasping, heavy with apparent relief.

Emery blinked in mild surprise. She was awake, with all of her faculties more or less intact, and Drake Tallen actually looked as if he cared. He looked as if he'd been worried. She put a hand to her forehead where it was pulsing painfully and decided that the small bump and scrape she found must have something to do with it. She'd had a nasty blow to the head, been knocked into temporary oblivion, and now she was probably seeing things. "Are you sure?"

He smiled briefly and sat down beside her, brushing a stray lock of hair from her face. "Well, let's see." He let his hand drop to her throat. His fingertips were cool when he touched her. Cool and smooth and strangely soothing. "That does feel like a pulse. A little fast, maybe, but I'd say it's pretty certain you're alive. As for being conscious . . ." His eyes scanned her slowly, possessively, as if the cryptic emerald depths could call up every full, feminine curve from memory. "I can prove that to you as well. But it's going to require a different—technique."

But Emery didn't need any further convincing. She was fully awake now, and her brain was beginning to fire back messages that had nothing to do with any dream state. Multiple, immediate, and clearly physical messages. Drake beside her, touching her, with only the bedcovering between them. His bedcovering. His hands. His bed.

She struggled to sit up. "Where am I?" But she knew the question was rhetorical. Her situation was obvious. Unthinkable. She was hurt and helpless and lying in her ex-lover's bed.

"Lie down, you little fool. Unless you'd like me to tie you down."

Her head hit the pillow in seconds. Not that she responded so easily to Drake Tallen's imperious orders. It was just that her body didn't seem to want to stay vertical by itself. She glared up at him, frustrated. "There. I can hardly move, anyway. Are you satisfied?"

"Let's just say I'm reassured. You need rest. You nearly killed yourself out there."

"There were *bats*," she said, shuddering. "They were after me."

"They were after *insects*," he explained. "They usually swarm this time of night. You just happened to be in the way."

"How inconsiderate of me."

"How foolish, Em. Do you always close your eyes when you run?"

"Only when I'd rather not look. What did I hit anyway, a brick wall?"

"A tree," he answered, and added dryly, "but don't worry, it's still standing."

Emery picked up the nearest pillow and swatted him with it. "Very funny. You haven't completely lost your sense of humor."

Drake wrested the pillow from her easily. A little too easily, in his opinion. She was weak from the accident. Physically hurting because of him. The one thing he'd never wanted to happen.

She was wrong about his sense of humor. He'd lost it all right. The second he'd come close to losing her. Again. God, but his heart had nearly stopped when she'd passed out cold in front of him.

She'd been a feather in his arms when he'd carried her inside. But the icy weight of a bone-chilling fear had made his entire body go numb. He'd been barely able to lay her on her back to make sure she was still breathing. Barely able to cleanse her forehead, keep her warm, and keep breathing himself.

But it had worked itself out in the end, hadn't it? She hadn't managed to run away from him after all. Hadn't managed to escape. No, it wasn't exactly what he'd intended, but he couldn't deny being pleased with the result. She was fine except for a few bumps and bruises. And she was still with him. In his home. In his bed.

She was right where he wanted her.

"Try to get some sleep," he suggested.

"What?"

"Sleep," he repeated calmly. "Rest. Shut-eye. The second best thing to do in bed. It's easy, pet. Just close your eyes."

"Impossible," she said flatly. "I am *not* staying here. I can't!"

He lifted his eyebrows at her. "Can't or won't?"

"It's simply out of the question," she told him, stubborn as always.

Age hadn't mellowed that about her, Drake decided. It had amplified it. No wonder she'd survived the recent accident so well. Her head was too strong for a little thing like a thirty-foot oak tree to make a dent in.

God help the man who ever actually did manage to marry her. He was going to need every ounce of his strength just to keep Ms. Emery Brooks in line.

"Tasha will worry," she added. "She's expecting me at her house."

"No problem," he countered. "I'll give her a call. I'm certain she'll understand. In fact, I'm sure she'd agree you should rest. Right where you are."

Drake could see her resolve weakening, further proof that she wasn't feeling one hundred percent herself. Emery rarely gave up so easily. She rarely gave up without getting what she wanted.

But then, neither did he.

He saw the opportunity to win due to her temporary weakness and took it. "If you haven't been to the house yet, you probably still have your suitcase in the car. Toothbrush, soap, whatever's required for spending the night. Maybe a flannel nightgown that buttons all the way up to your ears? Why don't I just hop on Stealth and go get it for you?"

She shot him a suspicious glance. "Where—where would you sleep? I mean, I don't suppose you have a guest bedroom."

Drake eyed her in amusement. So she was con-

cerned about the forced intimacy of their surroundings, was she? Well, that made two of them.

"Worried about what might happen?" he asked.

She folded her arms across her chest and stared
up at the tent ceiling, doing her best not to look at
him. "No. Of course not. I—I'm just—curious."

"Curious?" he repeated. "If I recall correctly,
your *curiosity* is what got us into trouble before."

She turned back toward him, looking angrier
than he'd expected. "Trouble is being forced to
leave your hometown for ten years. If we made a
mistake back then, believe me, *I've* already paid for
it."

Drake frowned at her reaction. Where had all
that explosive emotion come from? What right did
she have to be so angry? *He* was the one who'd been
jilted.

Wasn't he?

"No one forced you to leave, Em. It was your
choice."

"Right," she said bitterly. "Just like it was your
idea to marry me."

Drake shook his head in confusion. What was
she getting at? No, it hadn't been his idea. But he'd
done the right thing by her when it had mattered
the most. He'd accepted the consequences of his ac-
tions and honored his obligation to her. At least,
he'd tried.

"I'd never have shown up at the ceremony if I
didn't intend to go through with it," he told her.
"*You're* the one who backed out."

"Yes," she agreed, "I was. But I thought you'd be happy about it!"

Drake remembered thinking the same thing himself, once. He should've been ecstatic that she'd let him off the hook. He'd been sorry instead.

"Em," he said softly, "what made you believe that? What more could I have done to prove my intentions were honorable? Didn't I agree to get married?"

She sat up in bed then, wincing as she folded her arms across her chest. "Yes, you *agreed* to it. And what a noble gesture it was. An incredible *sacrifice* on your part, since you were still in love with my sister! You should consider yourself lucky for never having to make it."

"Pet," he persisted, trying to keep his voice calm in spite of Emery's escalating emotions. In spite of his own. "You knew how I felt about Tasha. I took it pretty hard when she came home married to that goon." He gave her a slow grin. "I was insulted, actually. I couldn't believe she picked that guy over me. It wasn't my heart that was bruised. It was my ego."

"I hope it *hurt*," she breathed softly.

Drake frowned again. There was something Emery wasn't saying to him. Something they both needed to get out in the open. He tucked a hand under her chin, forcing her to meet his gaze. "Why, Em?" he demanded. "Wasn't what *you* did to me painful enough?"

"I left because I had to," she said, her eyes wide

with unshed tears. "I couldn't marry you, not after—after what happened. Don't you understand? I *heard* you and Tasha talking at the church."

Drake blinked in surprise. She had heard—what? A sudden wave of guilt washed over him as a dim cloud of memory crystallized into sudden comprehension. Oh hell, he *had* said something to Tasha, just before the "Wedding March" had begun. Some idiotic profession of undying love, as far as he could remember. He'd probably meant it at the time, but he'd clearly made a moronic fool of himself. It was amazing what hormones could do to a man at that age. Yes, hormones. That's all it had been with Tasha.

But as badly as he'd been wounded by Ms. Tasha Brooks, the man-eating love goddess, it seemed that little sister Emery had suffered a few scars of her own. Was *he* the one responsible for them? Had she really bolted because of the cruel conversation she'd overheard?

"Aw, Em," he groaned, shaking his head. "Why didn't you say something to me? You might've slapped my face, at least, brought me back to my senses."

She glared at him, her expression hurt, unforgiving. "I was wearing the engagement ring you'd bought for *her*. Didn't *that* say it all?"

Drake felt as if she had slapped him, then. Just the look on her face hit him hard, gripping somewhere low in his gut. Had he always been such a sucker for those sad brown eyes of hers? They were enormous, soft and weepy, strangely sensual in their anger, searing him straight through to his soul.

"I pawned my truck to buy that ring, pet," he explained gently, "pitiful as it was. Tasha never even *saw* it. I had that to give you, or nothing at all. I could never have afforded another."

"It doesn't matter now," she told him, sniffing, appearing only slightly mollified by the brutal sincerity of his story. "At least we were both saved from making the biggest mistake of our lives."

Was she right? Drake wondered. Would it have been a mistake?

Probably.

But marrying Tasha would've been an even bigger one. At least he and Emery had been friends. He'd *liked* her, which was more than he could say for her self-centered older sister.

He and Em might have had a chance, or at least as good a chance as any marriage has. He'd seen his mom and dad fight for years before they'd finally called it quits. He'd sworn he would never get married and make the same mistakes. Until he'd fallen for Tasha.

He'd had nothing to offer her. He'd been broke, in debt big-time from college loans, with a blue-collar job that provided little or no security. She'd wanted stability. She'd found it in the form of Milton Matthews, a dull, balding college math professor with a safe, steady bank account.

She was still married to the man, which Drake could barely care less about after all this time. But the apparent success of her marriage, or any marriage for that matter, was something he considered close to a minor miracle.

He simply didn't believe in happily ever after any longer. How could he, after all the false promises that "legal" love had given him? The divorce of his own parents, Tasha's elopement, and the final straw, Emery's frantic escape from a shotgun wedding *he'd* been forced into. No, Drake Tallen and the idea of marriage definitely didn't mix.

He was a man on his own, and long past imagining his life would work any other way. A man with no ex-wives, no children to fight for custody over, and no regrets.

Except one.

Emery Brooks. He'd brought her back here to get some answers and to put the past behind them. He'd discovered something different instead.

He wanted her. Not as the innocent, almost virginal young bride she'd been. But as the strong, defiant, determined woman she'd become.

Oh yes, he definitely wanted her. Not professionally, to evaluate his stone, but physically, to ease the empty ache she'd started inside him. The ache she'd left him with at the altar all those years ago.

He wanted her here, now, in any way she cared to name. In every erotic, exciting way he could imagine.

"Go to sleep, Em," he told her, forcing himself to stand up from the bed and slowly walk away. "Before any more mistakes are made tonight. Before

I'm tempted to do something else we would both regret."

Emery woke early. Maybe because she wasn't used to sleeping in a strange, exotic cavern with Drake Tallen less than twenty feet away from her on his couch. Not that she wanted to get used to it. Her head was still a little sore, but her body felt much better after a night of rest. She felt fine, in fact. Strong enough to leave.

Still clad in the T-shirt he'd tossed her the night before, she tiptoed out of the tent and started rummaging through her suitcase for some fresh clothes. At least Drake had been civilized enough to retrieve her belongings before going to bed, although he'd barely said two words to her in the process.

"Right" had been one of them, when she'd sworn she hadn't packed a single flannel nightgown, insisting she usually slept in the raw. It'd been a lie, of course, but the thought of him being so correct about her choice of bedclothes was simply too annoying to confess. And although she was normally far from vain, she'd rather die than don her favorite faded, baggy blue *flannel* jams in Drake's bed.

"Here" had been his second word, when he'd handed her one of his shirts to sleep in, an oversized sack of coarse, no-nonsense cotton that nearly reached her knees. Not exactly fashionable, or as completely opaque as she might've liked, but definitely better than nothing.

Had the gesture been a peace offering, she wondered, or was Drake just displeased with the prospect of her bunking down in the buff? It was hard to tell since he hadn't glanced her way again since she'd slipped it on.

Until now.

"What are you doing up at this hour?"

She turned to see him watching her from the sofa, studying her at his leisure, languidly observing her every move. Just how long had he been awake, she wanted to know, and exactly what did he find so interesting? Was it the rumpled shirt or the wild, mangy "morning hair" that held his fascination? Or were there other parts of her showing that shouldn't be?

She folded her arms across her chest, instinctively defensive. "I'm trying to get dressed. Would you mind turning around?"

But Emery knew she was the one who should never have looked. Even in the morning, Drake was still the sexiest man she'd ever seen. Make that *especially* in the morning. After a full night of sleep, there was hardly a hair out of place on his dark, irreverently handsome head. Just that one wave streaking defiantly down his forehead in a slim, jagged line.

And for someone who didn't believe in sleeping in the nude, he was surprisingly close to doing just that himself. From the waist up, he wore nothing at all. Nothing except those tightly coiled masses of sleek, serious muscle and the warm, sexy tone of a deep summer tan. That, and a pair of intense emerald eyes with an expression of such shocking, sensual brilliance, they could mesmerize with a single glance.

No wonder the locals stood in such awe of him. Drake Tallen had more pure, powerful, animal magnetism than any mortal male should be allowed to have. Not to mention a will of his own and a mind as boldy independent as his wild, warrior ancestors.

He apparently had no intention of turning around. He stood up from the couch instead, revealing exactly what he had on below the waist. Shorts, thank goodness. Silky, black, waist-baring boxer shorts. Better than nothing, Emery reasoned, but only just. He stretched himself out and came toward her.

The three dogs Emery'd seen the day before began to stir from their resting place on the floor. They'd been curled up so quietly in a single, silent pile, she'd nearly mistaken them for a furry, overstuffed ottoman. The largest one still kept his distance from her, wary of the strange woman who'd invaded his den, but the smallest, a thin, streamlined greyhound, padded up to her cautiously, his tail tucked between his legs, and pressed a cold nose to her hand.

"Hi, there," Emery said softly, stroking him gently between the ears. "What's your name?"

"That's Rowdy," Drake said gruffly.

"Rowdy?" Emery questioned, looking down doubtfully at the friendly animal. "You don't look so rowdy to me," she told the soulful-eyed dog as his tail began to wag.

"You'd be surprised," Drake answered dryly. "These three were pretty good at getting into trouble before I took them in. Roaming the suburban streets like a pack of wolves. Terrorizing neighborhood children. Going through everyone's garbage."

Rowdy blinked up at her sorrowfully, his face a picture of mute, mongrel innocence.

"Rough's the big one," Drake continued, finishing the introductions, "and that's Jack over there."

She followed his gaze to the sleek, statuesque animal who stood nearby, his dark, intelligent eyes taking in every word his master uttered. Emery was reminded of a gorgeous Egyptian sculpture she'd once seen at the natural-history museum, representing a beautiful black jackal, tall, dark, and elegant.

"Jack," she repeated quietly, watching the animal's ears prick forward at the sound of his name. "He's the handsome one," she decided out loud.

"Careful," Drake warned her, his tone softly teasing, "or the rest of the pack might get jealous."

Emery smiled. "The pack? Does that include you?"

"It does," he admitted, laughing. "At least *they* believe I'm the lead dog." He sent the three of them off to the kitchen then with a single command. "See what I mean?" he said. "It's amazing how well they obey me when they know breakfast is on the way."

Emery laughed with him, and for a moment her mind screened back to an earlier time when she and

Drake had been together. They'd been comfortable in each other's company, once. She'd been happy just to be with him. But so much had changed since that sweet, sultry summer, she knew they could never go back. No matter how much she might want to.

"The bathroom's this way," he said, breaking into her thoughts, taking her by the arm. "Can you walk?"

She wondered briefly what he would do if she told him she couldn't. Carry her? "I'm fine, thank you. Much better." She quickly scooped up her morning essentials and let him lead her to the entrance.

But the washroom, like the rest of Drake's home, wasn't at all what she'd expected. It wasn't a tiny nook hollowed out from the stone walls just to house the shower and toilet. It was a lush, green, air-perfumed glen, complete with a steaming spring pool, just big enough for two people to bathe in. The edges were overgrown with feathery forest ferns, the stone floor carpeted with soft, spongy moss that felt like bliss beneath Emery's bare feet.

"Towels are over there," he said, indicating a plush pile stacked against the far wall. "Take your time," he added, and left her alone again, closing the door behind him.

As soon as Emery undressed and lowered herself gently into the hot water of the pool, she resolved to take Drake up on his offer. The sensations of the steam and the heat, and the sweet, oxygen-rich smell of the plants were enough to keep her soaking there for hours. Or at least long enough to wash every lingering trace of bat breath and tree bark from her overwrought body. She closed her eyes, letting the warm, lapping waves of the spring float away the last remnants of tension.

A can opener sounded somewhere in the kitchen and she heard the dogs barking loudly in excitement. She grinned at the idea of Drake Tallen, so tough and independent, taking in a bunch of wild stray mutts. It was that soft spot in his heart she'd first fallen in love with. The part of him that had looked after a sick, elderly grandfather and stayed with him until the end. The part that fought against the quarry owners and had always been on the side of the underdogs, even now that he was the top dog himself. The part he was normally too proud to show to the rest of the world.

When she came out half an hour later, he was waiting for her, leaning against the kitchen counter, polishing off a mug of coffee. Emery was relieved to see he'd put on a robe over those silky shorts. Unfortunately, the stupid thing didn't have any buttons, and she could still see a lot more of that magnificent chest than she really wanted to. She could see it was still as hard and smooth as dense, die-struck metal, crowned with just a sparse scattering of hair.

The dogs had cleaned their bowls and disappeared, probably out for a morning run. Drake himself looked ready to get on with the business of the day. At least he didn't waste any time getting down to it. He put a hand in the pocket of his robe, pulled out a small glittering object and rolled it toward her across the counter.

In spite of the careless way he handled it, Emery knew immediately what it was. The infamous stone. The Devil's Diamond. And the seeming source of all her recent trouble. After everything that had happened so far, she was almost afraid to touch it.

"Go ahead," he told her. "Check it out. It's what you came for."

Yes, Emery reminded herself. And that was still the most important thing, wasn't it? Doing her work well. Remembering exactly what her mission was. Somehow, she'd been temporarily distracted by all the unresolved emotions that had surfaced between them. But she was calmer now, more clearheaded. And her professional curiosity was piqued.

Stepping forward, she picked up the gem. And felt a sudden rush of excitement just from holding such a treasure in her hand. It was thrilling, she had to admit, to examine what was clearly the most spectacular stone she'd ever laid eyes on.

"Wow" was the only thing she could think of to say.

Drake nodded, his expression empathetic. "Not bad, is it?"

"It's amazing," she agreed. "Textbook shape. Incredible color. *Wow.*"

He pulled out a stool for her at the counter. "Sit down. I don't want you passing out on me again."

She didn't argue. She took the seat he'd offered, still clutching the diamond in her hand, feeling like a kid who'd just found the golden Easter egg. She held it up to the overhead light, trying to catch a glimpse of what was inside. No flaws were visible to the naked eye. Nothing but cool, ocean-green color beneath a layer of frosty whitecaps. "Have you louped it?" she asked excitedly. "Found any flaws at a higher magnification?"

Drake shrugged. "I thought I'd leave that up to you. I brought your equipment in earlier." He nodded toward the thick aluminum case that was stowed at the end of the counter. "You can set it up right here."

Emery didn't waste a minute retrieving her microscope from its well-padded container. Plugging the long cord into the nearest electrical outlet, she adjusted the eyepieces and carefully placed the diamond in the double-pronged stoneholder. She watched the crystal's interior glow bright as she flipped on the light switch, then settled herself in to take a closer look.

She saw nothing but an unbroken, breathtaking field of smooth glacier green. Nothing but brilliant, impenetrable beauty. No inclusions, no feathers, no flaws.

It was perfect.

Almost *too* perfect.

She forced herself to blink a few times, then take a second glance. But no matter how thoroughly she searched, the results were still the same. The stone was eerily free of a single, internal blemish or fault.

It was flawless.

Her eyes met Drake's over the top of the microscope. "Where did you find this?"

"Indian Creek," he said, pouring two more cups of coffee and sliding one to her across the counter. "You know the place."

"Oh." Emery lowered her gaze back to the eyepieces, unable to hold Drake's pointed glance any longer. Indian Creek. Yes, she did know the place. But only because it was *the* place. The spot where they had spent that one night in each other's arms.

She'd lost her heart along the banks of that stream. The same stream where Drake discovered the diamond. How often had he been there during those interim years? she wondered. How often had he thought of that night himself? At this moment she wasn't sure she wanted to know.

Willing the questions to the back of her mind, she directed her attention to the task at hand. Analyzing the diamond. It was flawless, she'd already determined that. But there was something else about it that seemed a little strange. A velvety, half-seen halo that clung like a misty cloud along its outer edges. The stone definitely had an odd aura about it.

An aura? That sounded a little too occult for her own comfort, a little too creepy for objective observation, but she knew her eyes weren't deceiving her. She also knew there had to be a sound, logical, scientific explanation for the phenomenon.

Of course there was. Stones didn't glow like that for no good reason. There were tests that would quickly dispel any trace of myth or magic. Comforting tests she'd expertly executed a thousand times.

In this case, the blacklight would likely reveal an immediate answer. The rays from a fluorescent bulb could often make a diamond glow. Pale blue was the usual color, and exactly what Emery expected to see when she turned the instrument on. But first the room would have to be completely dark.

"Mind if I turn off the lights?" she asked. "I'd like to check the fluorescence."

Drake flipped a switch on the nearby wall and the cavern was flooded in darkness. Such pure, mind-boggling black, Emery couldn't see her hand in front of her face. But she could hear him beside her, standing over her, waiting to watch the results for himself. She could feel his slow, steady breathing against the back of her neck, smell his raw masculine scent all around her.

Fumbling with the blacklight, she managed to locate the correct button and turn the instrument on.

The results of her test were immediate. She'd been right. The diamond was fluorescent, which easily explained the aura. But it didn't glow the usual bright blue. The Devil's Diamond burned red in the dark. A luminous, mystifying, unearthly blood red.

Drake laughed softly. "Fascinating, isn't it? That's one of the more—unusual properties of the gem. It lights up like magic. Black magic, that is. Or in this case, crimson. Either way, it's a hard one to explain."

Emery hesitated, a little too cautious to instantly accept what she saw. It wouldn't do to jump to any crazy conclusions. Her scientific training simply wouldn't allow it.

Granted, the outcome was very weird. The eerie red glow did make the formerly green diamond seem a little ghoulish. Almost preternatural. But that color of fluorescence wasn't completely unheard of in certain stones. And she didn't want to assume it was a sign of anything strange. Another clue to the curse, for instance.

"Not at all," she insisted. "Sound scientific principles are at work here." She pushed the stone a little closer to the light, still observing the visual data with as much detachment as possible. "In this case," she continued, "it's simply a result of the properties of this particular diamond reacting to the different wavelengths of light. It's caused by certain chemical particles within the matrix of the crystal structure."

"So it's chemistry?" Drake asked quietly behind her.

"Chemistry," she agreed.

She felt his hand stroking along the length of her hair. "Sometimes chemistry's not such a simple thing to figure out."

Emery closed her eyes, trying to clarify what was happening. Outside it was morning and the sun was shining. The deer were grazing in the forest. The crooked chimneys in the cozy country shacks were starting to smoke, warding off the early autumn chill. Life was calm, innocuous. Normal.

But she was here in the dark, alone with Drake Tallen in his luxurious underground labyrinth. She was here and he was way too close and her life was far from normal. One stroke from his hand and her world was starting to turn upside down. One touch from the devil himself and her insides were beginning to burn.

She ducked away from him, into the blackness, and scrambled blindly toward the switch on the wall. The lights flooded on. And her sanity quickly returned.

"I'll need some more information," she told him, pulling a notebook and pen from her equipment case and preparing to take down the details. "The stone's point of origin probably holds further clues to its unique peculiarities."

"No doubt," Drake answered dryly, almost amused by her sudden professional attitude. But she didn't fool him for a second. Ms. Businesslike Brooks was squirming inside, too frightened to face her own feelings. Determined to keep her distance. Well, that setup suited him just fine.

No problem, pet. He'd be more than happy to keep his hands off her. For the moment, anyway.

"Do you recall the geology associated with the area?" she asked in her most efficient, methodical voice. "The composition of the adjacent strata, any significant outcroppings or sedimentation?"

Hell, she had to be kidding. What Drake recalled about the area had nothing to do with the local rocks. It had far more to do with her body beneath his, with her hair splayed out against the blanket in soft, streaming rivulets, with the expression of wonder in her warm brown eyes when she finally exploded in his arms. He'd been back there a hundred times since and he doubted he could describe a single inch of the sediment. Sediment be damned. Didn't she remember the passion?

"Nothing significant," he told her.

"Hmmm . . ." She tapped the eraser tip of her pen along the edge of the counter, thinking hard.

But apparently not about the same thing he was. Not about that summer they'd spent together. Not about that night. When he'd mentioned Indian Creek, she'd barely reacted, as if she didn't remember.

Drake promised himself he was going to remind her.

"Was this particular octahedron the only one you identified? Were there any less significant stones found in the same location?"

"I wouldn't know. I didn't bother to look."

"You didn't bother to—are you saying there might be *more?*"

"It's possible."

Drake didn't miss that familiar gleam in her eyes. He knew exactly what she was thinking. She wanted to see the spot for herself. She wanted to feel the thrill of the search again, explore every wild, unknown acre of it the way they had once before.

A part of her was still that same eager, all-too-willing, wide-eyed kid. And there still might be a part of himself that was willing to oblige her. Back at the creek, the past wouldn't be so easy for her to forget. Back at that spot he vowed to *make* her remember.

FOUR

Emery couldn't resist the idea of it. Drake's land could be sitting on top of a fabulous diamond cache. But even if there weren't any other stones to be discovered at the site, the potential for scientific information was tempting enough. Besides the fact that her innate curiosity was killing her. She wanted the chance to check it out for herself.

Drake was the only catch. Once, his spirit of reckless adventure had been so strong, nothing would have stopped him from the search. Once, he would have called after her to join him and she'd have come running without a second thought. This time, she was the one who had to ask.

"Would you mind taking me out there to have a look?"

He cocked his head at her in curious speculation, arching his sinewed iron shoulders in a careless shrug. "We'd have to ride Stealth. The road's a little rough, but he's surefooted. And fast."

Stealth? Emery figured that was the name of the dreaded black stallion she'd had some experience with the night before. She didn't doubt for a second that the awesome animal could ride like the wind. It was easy to picture Drake sitting astride him, straining forward for speed, his black hair whipping, muscles in motion, until the two dark creatures became one. She just didn't want to imagine herself there, too, hanging on for all she was worth, hugging Drake's back tighter than an Indy 500 car around a curve. And even though she hadn't been alone on horseback in a long, long time, going it solo still seemed a lot safer.

"Haven't you got something nice and slow in that corral of yours?" she asked him hopefully. "Something very old and tame I might be able to ride myself? A senile Shetland pony, for instance?"

He gave the request a moment's consideration, then shot her an easy nod. "There's a gelding that should be gentle enough if you prefer to ride alone. Meet me outside in fifteen minutes. I'll have him saddled up."

"Him?" she asked in sudden concern. "Don't you mean them? You're going with me, aren't you?"

A faint hint of a smile crept into the corners of his mouth. "I wouldn't miss it. But Stealth and I usually go bareback."

"Oh," Emery breathed. "Fifteen minutes, then. I'll get my gear."

Half an hour later they were on their way, with Drake's stallion taking the lead and Emery's calmer gelding, Grey, trotting comfortably behind. The morning was crisp, sharp, and sunlit as the final sweet remnants of the summer gradually gave way to autumn. A soft breeze swept across the valley, rustling the leaves overhead, tugging gently at Emery's hair until several wayward strands pulled loose from their confining clips. Her heart lifted right along with them, her emotions running freer than she'd allowed them to be in a very long time.

This heady kind of excitement was far different from the careful structure she'd accustomed herself to at Swank's. In Chicago, she rose at daybreak to dress and prepare for the day's demanding schedule over breakfast on the run. Her work was hectic, but well worth it. It was satisfying, challenging, and a boost to her ego to be good at something. But, busy as she was, she rarely had a chance to take in the richness of the day around her. Gratefully, she took it in now.

If her riding skills were slightly rusty, Grey didn't seem to mind. Neither did she. She was a girl again, experiencing something far too easily lost during the trials of adulthood. The sensation of simple, uncomplicated joy.

Drake glanced back at her, apparently checking on her progress. His hair was tousled by the breeze, gleaming in the sun. Emery felt the dull sense of longing throb deep within her stomach at the sight.

It was only natural, she rationalized, for a woman

to be drawn to him. His posture was proud, poised for action, as confident and commanding as his ancestors must've been millennia ago. He was so supremely male, it would've been abnormal of her *not* to notice.

It was a scientific reaction, she told herself, the same kind of appreciative observation she made when checking out some magnificent rock. Physically, Drake Tallen was ideal. If she were grading him for imperfections as impersonally as she might grade a gemstone specimen, she'd have to find him flawless.

He was simply too handsome for his own good. Or hers.

She'd never had the confidence to believe she was pretty enough to keep him. Not at seventeen. Not even now. Drake was the kind of man women wrote their phone numbers on the backs of matchbooks for. Along with their fax numbers, their E-mail addresses, and the quickest route to reach their apartments.

How could she compete with that? The last time anyone had tossed an address her way, it'd been a traffic cop, giving her written directions on where to mail the citation money.

No, she and Drake were so completely mismatched, it was better they hadn't married. His interest in her would never have lasted. Her self-esteem would never have survived.

"Almost there," he called back, breaking into her thoughts with his smooth velvet voice, seductive, yet trimmed with steel. "It's an easy ride the rest of the way."

They rounded a bend in the trail just then, and the sloping banks of Indian Creek came gradually into view. Easy? Emery wondered. Nothing could have been harder than seeing that lazy, gurgling stream again and riding straight up to its edge as if nothing had ever happened there. As if the memories of two passionate young lovers weren't forever planted on that soft, grassy spot.

All of it was the same. The cool lapping of the water, the moist, earthy summer smell, the ripeness of the season all around them. Only she and Drake were different. And a peaceful, secluded patch of paradise wasn't enough to make them lose their heads this time.

Drake checked the stallion and turned to face her. "Is anything wrong?" he asked softly, seeming to comprehend the disconcerted expression that was etched across her face.

"Nothing," she lied, meeting his curious gaze with an effort. Of course he didn't believe her. How could he when she didn't believe herself?

Okay, so she'd been set back for a second. What woman wouldn't be in the same situation? Didn't everyone remember that first, scary, sweet, exciting time? Didn't every woman want to venture to that point in her past again and lose herself in a moment of memories?

"Nothing much," she amended. "I was just . . . reminiscing."

"Reminiscing?" he asked with a slow, understanding smile. "Are you sure it wasn't something else? Fantasizing, for instance?"

"What?" she exclaimed, amazed at how easily he'd read the sensual direction of her thoughts. Amazed and slightly embarrassed. She wanted nothing more at the moment than to prove to him she was over all that. The out-of-breath attraction, the heart-melting schoolgirl crush. But at this rate she wasn't even sure she could convince herself.

Which meant there was only one clear, logical course of action to take. Bluff her way out of it. Banter him right back.

"You wish, Tallen," she told him, keeping her head high, her tone teasing. "More likely you're the one who's imagining things."

"Could be," he agreed, grinning in apparent appreciation of her saucy response. "But if you had any idea what sort of things, you'd probably slap my face."

"Don't tempt me," she shot back smoothly, congratulating herself on how cool and in control she sounded when her insides were actually sizzling from shock. Just what *was* he thinking? she wondered. Her face flushed pink at the possibilities.

But before she had a chance to consider them any further, her horse reared up, spooked by some small critter that had unexpectedly scurried across their path. Emery fought to hold on, but it wasn't any use. She slipped helplessly off of the animal's back, leaving Grey, the saddle, and her brassiness behind as she fell straight to the ground.

"Oomph!" The next thing she knew she was sprawled flat on her back in the densely packed dirt, struggling for air.

She heard Drake running toward her. Had he called out her name? She wasn't sure, but she decided there had to be an easier way to get his attention. Or at least a less humiliating one.

He knelt beside her. "Don't move," he commanded. "Hold still and try to catch your breath."

She didn't answer immediately. She couldn't. She was too busy gulping down oxygen, and Drake's sudden proximity certainly wasn't making it any easier. Just when she was regaining her composure, there he was, hovering over her, dark, dashing, *distracting*. Handsome enough to stop her heart on sight.

Going over every aching, bruised inch of her with his cool, competent hands.

"What are you doing?" she gasped.

"Checking you out for broken bones. Don't move. You're making it difficult."

Difficult? *He* was the one doing that, feeling her in places she doubted she even had bones, with a smooth, exploratory caress that would've been unspeakably insolent if her health hadn't been at stake. Come to think of it, she wasn't even sure if it was. "Do you have to touch me like that?"

"Rather be maimed for life, would you?"

"I'll take my chances," she said, attempting to sit up.

He pushed her back down. "Lady, you already take too many. Now, like it or not, I'm going to finish examining you."

"Over my dead body," she shot back, folding her arms across her chest.

"That can be arranged," he promised, firmly gripping her by the wrists and pinning both of her arms over her head.

Emery didn't bother to struggle. It was all too apparent which one of them was stronger. And with the kind of luck she'd been having lately, it probably wouldn't be any use. There *was* a curse on that diamond, she decided ruefully. A dangerous, near-deadly hex that seemed to be aimed directly against *her*.

How else could she explain the sudden streak of misfortune she'd been having ever since she'd laid eyes on him again?

Drake stared down at the woman beneath him, fighting for control of his emotions. He'd rushed to help her and found himself warring with her stubbornness instead. Damn Emery Brooks anyway, along with her infernal, impudent obstinacy. Didn't she know what was good for her? Didn't she know that he was good for her?

Apparently not, from the foolish way she was fighting him. If he had any sense, he'd let her go immediately, let her take her chances on risking further physical injury. But all those years at the jackhammer had clearly jolted every last shred of sense from his head long ago. Because he didn't want to let her go.

He wanted to shake her up, instead.

At the moment he could think of only one way to do it. Emotionally, Em seemed determined to remain just beyond his reach. She wasn't about to let him touch her there, not at the risk of being hurt again. But physically, she still lay within a few short inches. That was all the space that separated their bodies now. Ten years suddenly melted down to this second, to the few soft gasps that separated her tender, hot, half-open mouth from his.

Deliberately, Drake closed that last short space, and possessively put his lips on hers. He kissed her so roughly, it shocked them both.

A low groan escaped him. He forced his tongue inside, tasting the sweetness he'd never forgotten, probing so deeply he didn't think he'd ever find his way back. Her mouth opened willingly, taking all of him in at once, and she arched beneath him with an urgent, responsive whimper, wanting more.

Drake didn't stop to ask why. He gave it to her. He didn't stop to fumble with the buttons on her blouse. He tore it open, moving his mouth down to the sheer, silken fabric of her bra, dampening the lace and her breast beneath it as he lathed the filmy surface with his tongue. He felt her writhing in response, felt her nipple tauten as he ripped the lace off with his teeth and drew the wet, hardened tip between his lips.

She gave a soft cry, confused, excited. Yes, definitely excited. The sound of it left him hard beyond belief. He let go of her arms then, freeing his other hand to pleasure her. Unzipping her jeans, he shoved her panties aside and started to do just that.

She was softer than he remembered. Soft and smooth and exquisitely deep, as moist and mysteriously inviting as the damp, forbidden entrance to some dangerous, water-filled cave. The kind of place a man was compelled to seek out in spite of the hidden risks.

Drake wasn't gentle. His battering was swift, certain, insistent. His fingers moved inside her with the same sudden fierceness he felt in his heart.

To his surprise, she didn't attempt to push him away. Instead she drew him closer, weaving her fingers wildly through his hair, slipping her other hand up under his sweater to rake her nails slowly along the length of his back.

"Oh, God," she whispered.

But Drake knew that nothing short of heaven could help either of them now. He wanted her again, more than ever. He wanted her this moment, right here in the dirt, with only the sun above as silent witness. He hadn't known how much until he'd touched her. Oh, hell, he should never have touched her.

With an effort, he drew his hand away.

Emery didn't immediately understand why Drake had stopped. She only knew she didn't want him to. If he'd asked, she'd never have allowed him to touch her that way, but he hadn't asked.

He'd taken.

She knew he'd wanted to punish her for walking out on him, to even an old score. But they'd settled all that in the cave yesterday and he'd finally understood the reason she'd run away. So this wasn't about revenge any longer. And explanations weren't what he'd wanted just now.

He'd wanted *her*.

She sat up, struggling to pull her torn bra back in place, covering it with a blouse she could no longer button. Her hands were shaking so badly, she could barely manage to tie the front tails together, western-style. But the condition of her shirt was the furthest thing from her mind, because all she could think about was the way he made her feel. He'd left her with a slow, burning ache inside her belly, a sense of loss and longing so strong and bittersweet she could barely breathe.

"Something tells me that what just happened here hasn't got a thing to do with my health," she said softly, making a weak attempt at humor, "because I don't think I'm feeling much better."

"Dammit all, Em." He raked a hand roughly through his hair in apparent frustration. "I didn't intend for this to happen. At least, not like *that*."

That made two of them, Emery decided regretfully. Some professional she was, falling to pieces in the arms of the man she'd been sent to negotiate with. Talk about letting the seller have the upper hand. She'd been ready to give him much more than that. Hands, lips, body, just about anything he was willing to take.

"No doubt you were swept away by my irresistible charms," she answered wryly.

He scanned her face swiftly with intense, all-seeing eyes. They were the eyes of a mysterious sorcerer who could see straight into her soul.

"Is that so hard to believe?" he asked her.

"Yes," she responded truthfully. "I'm not Tasha, remember? Men aren't in the habit of swooning at my feet. I'm not beautiful, but at least I can be realistic about it."

"Realistic," he repeated, shaking his head. "Is that what you call it? Em, you must be blind."

"My eyes are working just fine," she insisted. "I know what I see when I look in the mirror."

He put a hand out to touch her face. His fingertips were infinitely tender this time, his stroking subtle, featherlight. "Ah, yes, your eyes. But are they all you can see with?"

Emery blinked in surprise, thrown off balance by his sudden empathy, by his gentle caress. "I—I'm not sure what you mean."

"Shut them," he told her.

"What?"

"Close your eyes and tell me what else you can see." He drew his hand across her eyelids, encouraging her voluntary compliance.

Slightly confused, Emery obeyed. "I don't see anything."

"Not even blackness?"

She hesitated. "Well, yes, that."

"What about color? What about your favorite color? Can you see it?"

A vibrant field of spring-green grass leaped suddenly to her mind. A soft, verdant landscape of peaceful, new-mown pasture. It was so real, she could almost imagine running barefoot through it, almost smell the sweet, familiar scent of a freshly cut lawn. Almost.

His voice cut into her thoughts, deep and compelling. "Where are you, Em?"

Her eyes flashed open. "I did see something. It was . . . beautiful."

"Beautiful?" he asked. "Even though it didn't take your eyes to discern it?"

She considered the question momentarily, puzzling over the point he was trying to make. Sight itself was only a single, isolated sense. Were there other ways of evaluating the world *and* herself she'd been consistently overlooking?

She shook her head slowly, still unsure about this new insight. Clearly she and Drake saw things very differently. So which one of them was right? "But it wasn't *real*."

Drake's smile was faint, enigmatic. "So if you can't confirm it externally, it doesn't exist?"

"No, I—I don't know. It was just a daydream. Just something I conjured up in my imagination."

"A vision," he corrected. "A place your own inner spirit took you to for a reason." He dropped his hand to her chest, resting his palm over her heart. "It's here, pet," he told her. "Inside you. What your inner guide shows you about yourself is far more important than anything the mirror could reveal. You just have to learn to look in a different way."

"I'm not sure I understand."

He drew his hand away and glanced across the dancing stream of Indian Creek, as if the far banks held some secret he wanted to share with her—some insight that might help her find the way. "You spend all your time looking for flaws, Emery. Searching for imperfections. Maybe you need to change your focus, start figuring out what's right instead. If beauty is what you're searching for, maybe you've merely been looking in the wrong place."

She took in the words slowly, letting the unfamiliar ideas sink in before letting out a long sigh. "I've been conditioned to see life that way. I'm a trained scientist, remember? I'm not *allowed* to believe in something there's no physical evidence for."

He turned back to face her with so much understanding in his empathetic eyes, Emery felt her heart squeeze tight.

"It's impossible to measure beauty, Em," he explained softly. "Whose yardstick are you going to use? What parameters are you going to set? There's no scientific formula that can help you find it."

She wanted to believe him. If what he said was really true, it would be such a relief. But she'd spent her entire life trying to fit things into neat, comfortable little categories. And she'd always known exactly which one *she* belonged in.

Average looks, better-than-average brains. The girl next door. Not even close to a sensual siren. And now he was suggesting the image she'd made for herself wasn't necessarily accurate? Not an easy leap of faith for someone who'd grown up in her gorgeous sister's shadow.

"If appearance is subjective, then how come everyone agrees about what's attractive and what isn't?"

"Everyone doesn't agree, despite the great societal pressure to conform. Tastes change, styles come and go from culture to culture. There's never been a consensus about what's beautiful since civilization began. Overweight bodies are a turn-on in some societies. Sumo wrestlers are heavyweight hunks in Japan. Pale skin was a sign of perfect virginal purity to the Victorians, while long, distorted earlobes or lips the size of saucers may be the ultimate in Borneo. It just depends on your point of view."

"Lips the size of saucers?"

"Not a personal favorite for me, but it probably has quite an effect on Bornean males." He brushed a strand of hair from her face, curling the stray lock leisurely around his long fingers. "I'm more into autumn-colored hair myself."

Emery's breath caught. She looked away, suddenly shy, feeling seventeen again and emotionally overwhelmed by Drake Tallen's erotic attention. Was it possible he really did think she was pretty?

Had he recognized something beautiful inside her during his slow, intimate explorations?

She'd never have accepted the idea ten years ago, but now there were parts of herself she actually liked. Inner strengths she'd worked hard at developing. Maturity itself had brought her a certain amount of self-confidence, but the biggest boost to her self-esteem had come from her work. She was good at what she did. It was her greatest source of personal pride.

At the moment Drake was distracting her from it. One heated kiss, one intimate conversation, and he'd made her forget her purpose. One look in those lethal green eyes of his and she could hardly remember why she'd come here at all.

Her career, of course. *That* was her main goal. She couldn't allow herself to be sidetracked from it again. She still had an important task to perform for her determined employer. A diamond to deliver. A deal to seal.

She stood up, deftly untangling her hair from his hand. It didn't matter anymore what Drake Tallen thought of her appearance. He wasn't simply an old flame of hers, he was a business associate, an adversary it would be necessary to negotiate with sooner or later. And when they finally did negotiate for the sale of the stone, she still intended to win.

"I appreciate your concern," she responded, her voice calm, carefully polite. "I think you were right. No broken bones." As if to emphasize just how perfectly normal she felt, she slowly tested the strength of her legs, then cautiously flexed each arm, one at a time. "See? It's all in working order, in spite of the curse. But maybe we need to begin our discussion over that little green rock before anything else unexpected happens. What do you say we go back to the cavern and talk about a price?"

He rose from the ground, flicking the dirt from his clothes as he flashed her an easy smile. "Whatever you say, Em. But I think I'd better warn you about that curse before we go any further. You may want to reconsider buying the stone after you hear the whole story."

"Nice try," she said. "But I won't be deterred so easily. The publicity potential for your rock is pretty high no matter what kind of bad luck it brings. A diamond with a provenance—a history behind it—is usually worth more than one of unknown origin."

"This one's past is pretty sketchy," he explained, reaching into the opening of his shirt and withdrawing a small chamois bag, suspended from his neck by a black leather cord. He drew the bag open, tipped it upside down, and dropped the diamond onto his palm.

Emery stared at the sultry rock that was gleaming now in the sun, glinting at her like one of Lucifer's own eyes, still winking wickedly after being plucked from its socket. All along, Drake had been carrying it with him. No wonder the curse had followed them out there.

"According to legend," he told her, "a stone of

this perfect shape is said to make its owner stronger by focusing energy through the twin pyramids."

"Indian legend?" she asked, remembering the fascinating tales his grandfather used to tell about the land and air and forest spirits. Could the story of the diamond be traced back to the time when Indiana was still occupied by Indians?

"The tale probably started with one of the tribal storytellers," he said, "but there's no written record of it until after the turn of the century, in some of the local folklore. Do you remember one of the earlier diamond finds we'd always heard about around here? The Maxwell?"

"Sure," she responded. "That's the one that was found on Goss Creek, right? Around 1863?"

"Exactly," he said. "Maxwell found the stone on his farm, where the creek crossed it. It was around four carats and said to be of a greenish hue."

"Greenish?" Emery asked. "Sounds like your stone and his might've come from the same source. Especially since the Goss is one of the tributaries of Indian Creek."

"I'm pretty sure of it," he concurred. "Because there was a larger stone find, very close to the Maxwell farm, that was never reported. A find that was said to have been made by a tribal medicine man, a shaman who was somehow related to the great Chief Tecumseh himself. A green diamond, over twenty carats, in the shape of a perfect octahedron."

Emery felt a faint shiver snake down along the

back of her spine. "The Devil's Diamond? Your diamond?"

Drake nodded briefly. "I believe they're one and the same. They say the rock became a protective talisman to the high priest, as well as a powerful weapon against his enemies. Or anyone who tried to part him from it."

"Part him—oh! So how did you end up with it?"

"Simple fate," he explained. "The diamond was dropped back into Indian Creek, returned there after the shaman's death because it was believed to be unlucky for anyone but its owner. Folks were afraid of it."

Emery eyed him in amazement. "But you're not?"

He grinned back at her. "Why should I be? Think about it, pet. I'm the rightful owner now."

She nodded slowly. "I see your point."

"So, just how brave are you, Emery Brooks?" he inquired as a smooth hint of a smile crept suggestively into the curved corners of his mouth. "Do you still want to try and part me from my diamond even though it might be dangerous?"

By the time they arrived back at the cavern and ate a light lunch, Drake had decided what he had to do next. Unfortunately, the curse hadn't set Em back one bit. In fact she'd given him a substantial offer for the stone the second they walked through the door. She was still as determined as ever to have his diamond. And he was equally determined *not* to let her.

For both of their sakes. After all, she'd already had two minor accidents. There was no telling how dangerous that gem might be. And if it really was bringing her bad luck, he couldn't allow her to risk her safety any further.

Besides, he wasn't ready to part with the diamond at this point, not after the good luck it had clearly brought him. It had brought her back here, proving that his feelings for her hadn't disappeared. They'd grown stronger instead.

Exactly what he intended to do about those feelings was an entirely different matter. If he was wise, he would heed the warning of his inner spirit guide and send his pet packing. He would master the drumbeat of desire that had started to pound inside him and send her back where she belonged before things really started to get serious.

But he doubted she'd go so easily. If swarming bats and bucking horses hadn't scared her off so far, he didn't know what would. No, it seemed Em wasn't about to budge for anything less than a full-blown natural disaster.

Of course, that never-give-up attitude of hers was one of the traits he admired about her the most. Her willingness to take a risk, to keep on fighting, even when the odds were against her. *Admired?* Who was he kidding? Her toughness turned him on.

Tasha had never been that gutsy. Her biggest dilemma was whether or not a walk in the woods with him was going to mess up her manicure. Em, on the other hand, would've followed him over the quarry cliff if he'd dared her to, mainly because she'd always had more spirit than good sense. She'd been worth ten of Tasha, even though he'd been too young and lovesick to see it before.

He'd been blind. He'd blown it big time.

He'd fallen for the wrong sister.

Unfortunately, it was too late to set it straight now. Past time to make it up to Em and properly repent for his own poor judgment. The most he could do was make her realize she was still a desirable woman. A little too damn desirable as far as he was concerned.

But her self-image had suffered from the way he'd treated her back then. The conversation by the creek had convinced him of it. *She didn't believe she was beautiful.*

He had to do something to show her she was wrong. Something that would prove just how much a man might want her. A man like himself, for instance.

There was only one way he could think of. It was an ingenious plan, actually. Easy, straightforward, and elegant in its simplicity. It would solve both of his problems at the same time. She would know how much she meant to him. And she would give up on getting the diamond, forever.

Because as soon as Em heard what his proposal was, he knew she would never go for it.

Yes, Drake decided, the plan was flawless. In fact,

he was so confident it would work, he decided to put it into effect immediately. He settled himself comfortably onto the leather couch, propped his dusty shoes on the coffee table, and prepared himself for the inevitable battle.

"Sorry, pet," he said, turning toward Emery with a calm, apologetic expression on his face, the kind a man usually reserved for playing poker or other games of chance. In this case, Drake decided, the stakes were just as high.

"Sorry for what?" she asked, leaning one arm on the edge of his fireplace mantel and eyeing him expectantly.

"For having to disappoint you. I've decided not to sell."

"*What?*"

Drake felt himself smiling inwardly. She looked as if she were about to throw something at him. Fortunately there were no sharp objects in sight. Not that he blamed her. He had a good idea how high Swank's was willing to go for the stone. He just wanted to prove to her it wouldn't be enough.

"For money, that is," he amended, starting to enjoy himself. There was something incredibly sensual about Em when she was angry. The stubborn tilt of her chin, the animal flare of her nostrils, the fire inside her that could turn to passion with a single, well-executed kiss. Drake resisted the strong urge to take her by the wrist and tug her down onto his lap. He'd bet that would *really* get her steamed.

Come to think of it, it would probably send them both over the edge. For the moment Drake wanted to keep his edge. With a hellion like Em to contend with, he was going to need it.

"You must be out of your mind," she told him, throwing her arms up in frustration. "You must know I'd be willing to offer you a fortune for it. What more do you want?"

What more did he want? He wanted to carry her straight into the bedroom, onto his bed, and see if their technique had improved in ten years. It couldn't have been the earth-shattering meltdown he remembered it to be. She'd only been a shy kid at the time. Hell, he'd barely been much wiser himself.

But he couldn't allow himself to revive that memory, not at the risk of hurting Emery again. Not unless she understood this time exactly what the consequences would be.

He shrugged. "I'm still willing to part with the stone," he told her. "But I doubt you'll be willing to pay my price."

"Try me," she suggested.

"I might," he shot back, flashing a smile. "One more time."

Her jaw dropped open, her body froze in sudden shock. *Exactly, pet*, his eyes told her silently. *You're beginning to get the idea.*

"I beg your pardon?" she said, breathless.

"The terms are simple," he explained. "One night together is all I'm asking."

"One . . . *night?*"

"Together," he confirmed. "From sunset to sun-rise, to do as I please. You get the diamond and I get you out of my system for good. What do you say, Ms. Brooks? Do we have a deal?"

FIVE

Emery gaped at him, aghast. He couldn't be serious! This wasn't really happening to her. She must be imagining it all. The mushrooms from the salad he'd given her had probably been poisoned, or were hallucinogenic at the very least. What did they call that species of fungi that some Indians ate to gain spiritual insight? Peyote mushrooms, that's what they were! They would certainly explain the odd stirrings that had started in the pit of her stomach, the sudden quickness of her breath, the warm flush she felt spreading slowly across her face.

"Let me get this straight," she managed, in spite of all the strange, erotic symptoms she was experiencing. Hallucination or not, she needed to get the facts before jumping to any erroneous conclusions. Not to mention the erogenous ones. "You want me to sleep with you in exchange for the diamond?"

Drake leaned back against the couch cushions,

folding his arms behind his head and leveling her a long, appraising look. "Just so you do get it straight," he responded smoothly, "I doubt there'll be any *sleeping* involved."

Emery felt the flush migrating quickly from her face to the rest of her body, until every tender extremity was softly, vibrantly tingling. No, she definitely wasn't imagining this. The reaction she had to him, to the *idea* of having him, was far too familiar to be drug-induced. Just thinking about it made her feel a little faint. Because she knew what he wanted her to do, what he wanted to do to her.

On second thought, he was the one who had to be under the influence of mind-altering mushrooms. Did he really believe she'd make a bargain like that just to further her career? Did he think she would sell her body to Beelzebub himself, just to get her hands on that stone?

"You're joking, right?"

He cocked an eyebrow at her. "I promise you, I'm perfectly serious. I can have a contract drawn up, if you'd prefer written proof. It would probably make some fascinating reading, but my attorney's extremely discreet."

A *contract?* Her face went hot with indignant curiosity. She could only imagine what the terms would be. Complete physical surrender. No, with Drake, mere bodily surrender wouldn't be enough. He'd ask for all of her, mind and soul, the emotional as well as the physical. Far more than she was able or willing to give.

But of course, she wouldn't even consider signing such a document.

Would she?

She folded her arms across her chest, still leaning against the fireplace mantel for support. There was a part of her that still wanted him that way. Several parts of her, in fact. She couldn't deny what had happened between them by the creek this morning. But if she gave in to simple desire, she'd be doing it for all the wrong reasons. And no matter how much her career meant to her, no matter the amount of pride she had in her work, she would never go to such lengths for success.

Unfortunately, Drake didn't seem willing to wait around to hear her excuses. He stood up from the couch, crossed the distance between them in two strides, and began to persuade her to his way of thinking.

"No answer yet, Em?" he asked, forcing her up against the wall with his nearness, enfolding her waist with his hands. He lowered his mouth to her throat, tasting her there, lathing the surface of her skin in slow, melting strokes, taking her a little at a time. His lips parted to speak, his breath short, his voice guttural and raw from the effort to talk. "Maybe you'd prefer some physical proof. Maybe I should show you exactly how serious I am."

If Emery'd had any doubts about his intentions before, they were dispelled the second their bodies made contact. He was ready to fulfill the bargain now, in no uncertain terms. He was hard enough to take her, right there, up against the cold, rough rock, to fully collect on his shameless proposal.

She swayed toward him instinctively, drawn like a night bird into the soft shadow of his arms, attempting to fly, but helplessly trapped. She choked back a sound. If he kissed her again, the way he had by the stream, she'd be lost. But his mouth didn't move toward hers.

Instead, he worked his hot tongue languidly down the base of her neck, abrading her baby-soft skin with his five o'clock shadow. He parted her blouse and his lips found the cleft between her breasts. He kissed her there, in that tender, private spot, making her skin moist, her breathing quick and shallow. She arched her back, almost involuntarily, bringing their bodies even closer, whimpering softly for something she was afraid to name.

Lord, what was wrong with her? The offer he'd made was insulting. The least she should do was push him away and swear she wanted nothing to do with his dastardly deal. But she didn't even have the strength of will to do that! Heaven help her, but she *liked* it.

She felt herself trembling as the swirling in her belly grew faster, sweeter, until her insides burned with the bright shivery sensation. The scratch of his afternoon stubble against her skin was pain and pleasure all at once, coarse and teasing beside the warm, soothing wetness of his tongue. She strained closer to the source of all that excitement, needing more, physically asking for it. Agreeing to his terms in the most intimate, nonverbal way possible.

She had to stop now before either of them got the wrong idea. Because she couldn't afford to take the devil up on his bargain, not at the risk of losing her soul, or herself, again.

She swallowed the breath she was taking, determined to speak. "I don't want it," she whispered hoarsely. "Not like this. I don't want the diamond that badly."

She felt him tense and hesitate. Pushing him away became moot at that point. He'd already stopped ravishing her on his own. He held her at arm's length so his glittering green eyes could focus on her face.

Emery kept talking, flustered by his sudden scrutiny, by the passion that was still apparent in the heat of his expression. "I—you can't believe I'd be willing to *trade* myself for the diamond."

He continued to survey her slowly, possessively, as if the deal were already done and she was his for the entire evening. As if he intended to have her in every enchanting, erotic way a man could imagine. "Why not?" he finally asked. "It's an honest exchange."

"Honest?" she squeaked, wary of the molten, mesmerizing look in his eyes. "It's indecent!"

"Hopefully," he told her, amused. "At least, I promise to do my best to make it that way. Come on, pet," he coaxed, his voice as smooth and cool as fine wine. "Spend the night with me and you can do what you damn well please with the stone."

"Right," she responded, her own voice full of frustration. "As long as you can do whatever you damn well please with me!"

"That's the general idea," he agreed. "But perhaps you'd prefer to discuss the specifics?"

Specifics? Just when she was trying to guess what he meant, his head bent closer to hers and his mouth nipped lightly, taking her earlobe between his teeth.

Emery's legs threatened to give way beneath her, but luckily, he stopped before her knees began to buckle. He touched his lips to the opening of her ear, instead, and whispered soft, shocking words. Sinful, forbidden, exciting words that were meant to be murmured in the dark.

"I *can't*," she whispered back. "You're asking too much."

He pulled away from her again, his tone hoarse with arousal, heavy with heat. "I won't force you, Em. The choice has to be yours. And I guess you've already made it."

Force her? No, she knew he'd never do that. Actually, Drake was right. There was no longer a choice to be made. She simply couldn't sell herself, no matter how high the price.

"We're not kids now," she told him. "We have to consider the consequences."

Yes, Drake agreed silently, the consequences. Good thing she had reminded him of them at this moment. He'd known all along what her answer would be, but getting physical with Em had taken more strength than he'd imagined. It was harder than he had expected to hold himself back. Hell, *he* was harder than he'd expected.

Even though his brain had been so sure she'd say no, his body had been hoping for a yes.

A trickle of a tear appeared at the corner of her eye as she tore herself out of his grasp. "It would never work," she whispered.

Drake didn't think he could take it if she went all wet and weepy on him now. The urge to comfort her, to take her into his arms again, was almost too strong to resist. But she was right. It wouldn't work. At least, not for long. He'd sworn he wasn't going to make the same mistake twice with this woman, not when a long-term commitment was out of the question.

He'd vowed he wasn't going to hurt her again. Emery definitely deserved better than that—better than he. She deserved a man who still believed in the promise of love, in the sanctity of marriage. A man who believed forever was possible between the right people. Unfortunately, he wasn't that man.

And at the moment he'd had about all of the holding back he could handle. "If you don't plan to stay," he warned her, "you'd better leave now, pet. I can't promise how long I'll be able to keep my hands off you."

She nodded, wiping the moistness from her face with the back of her hand. Five minutes later she was gone.

———◆———◆———

Drake stood shirtless at the edge of the quarry cliffs, his body perfectly still. The balls of his feet were bare, firmly planted at the brink of a sixty-foot precipice. His muscles were coiled, ready for the descent into the dark waters below, but his mind had journeyed ahead already, moving to a higher plane, seeking the wisdom of his soul spirit guide.

It was a skill his grandfather had taught him long ago, a way to clear his mind and focus on the problems that had to be solved. And, he hoped, to find some answers. But the search was treacherous this time, requiring every ounce of his meditative energy.

He closed his eyes, summoning up his animal guide, following the swift bird's dark, darting wings on their unerring course of flight. Where would the nighthawk take him tonight? The creature was flapping swiftly, surely, maneuvering as lightly as a wind-borne leaf, challenging Drake to soar higher. Daring him to step over the edge.

But there were rocks below him, as well as water. This midnight dive would take all his concentration, his greatest leap of faith. Blind, perfect trust in his own inner instincts. Beneath the full harvest moon, into the cool shining waters, the hawk would show him the way.

With his eyes remaining shut, his torso sheened with sweat, he thought of her. Emery. The reluctant child-bride in a wedding gown of virgin white, the sensual, willful woman she'd become.

The problem was, he wanted her still. Even now, after he'd sent her away. The scent of her perfume softly clinging to his skin reminded him just how much. Her fragrance was hot, earthy, as full of spice and fire as the warm, windblown waves of her hair.

His plan had worked perfectly, dammit. He'd made his proposal crystal clear. She'd refused to go through with it, just as expected. She'd told him what he could do with his diamond. She was probably packing her bags at this moment, preparing to leave town again.

Which wasn't at all what he wanted.

But Drake wasn't sure what to do about that. He could only hope now that his spirit would guide him. All he had to do was follow the nighthawk into the darkness, to find the answer he sought on the other side.

All he had to do was fly.

He lifted his arms high over his head, flexing the muscles that had been stilled for so long, and launched himself into the sky.

"Did you get it?"

They were the first words out of Mia's mouth when Emery phoned from Tasha's house with the bad news. She'd tried to let her boss down easy by explaining the seller had changed his mind, but Mia simply wasn't ready to accept defeat.

"Nonsense," she insisted, the minute Emery had finished talking. "He'll sell if the offer's right. Everyone has their price."

Even Drake, Emery agreed silently. But in this case it was probably better not to fill her boss in on *all* the details, especially not Drake's asking price. Mia would gladly trade her employee's soul for the stone if given the opportunity. One night of . . . well, one *night* in exchange for the diamond of the decade would likely strike her as the bargain-basement deal of the century. Particularly since it wasn't *her* body that was being offered.

"It doesn't look good, Mia," she responded diplomatically. "We've reached an impasse in our negotiations." Actually, Emery mused, it was more like a major roadblock. Drake wasn't going to budge from his implacable position. And she wasn't going to give in.

No matter how much she wanted to.

Lord help her, but the most painful part was she *did* want to. Not for the diamond. Not for the sake of Swank's, or to further her career, but for herself. For both of them.

What better way to finally forgive Drake Tallen for the past? What better way to let go than to go back, and relive the night she'd first given him her love?

But of course, the very idea of it was completely out of the question. Just about as improbable as the idea of him selling her the stone for cold, hard cash instead of warm, steamy . . . No, the negotiations were over as far as she was concerned.

But "no" wasn't a word that Mia Swank understood. The woman simply had no experience at graciously accepting failure. She wanted that diamond and she didn't care how Emery got it.

"The man is toying with you," Mia told her. "Of course he still wants to sell. He's holding out to see if we'll up our offer. A very clever negotiating tactic on his part. You'll just have to stay there a little longer and wait it out."

Emery sighed. The message didn't seem to be getting through to Mia at all. Waiting wasn't going to work. Neither was raising the price. There was only one thing Drake Tallen would trade that rock for and that one thing wasn't for sale.

She still wasn't sure whether to be flattered by his offer or insulted. He was turning down a fortune just to sleep with her. Besides the fact that she couldn't comply, it was hard to comprehend that he thought she was worth it.

Maybe some other woman would be. Maybe someone as breathtaking as Tasha. But brown-eyed, wild-haired, plain-bodied her? She seriously doubted it.

"Of course, I'll hang around a bit longer if you'd like me to, Mia, but I honestly don't think it's going to do any good. The seller is . . . determined."

"Nonsense," Mia countered, her voice growing shrill. "Give him another two or three days, and if he doesn't budge, ante up an extra ten thousand.

That oughta put a dent or two in his determination."

"I'll try," Emery agreed. "I just don't want you to get your hopes up too high."

"*My* hopes aren't on the line here," her boss shot back, unperturbed. "If you don't come back with that diamond, you'd better *hope* you'll still have a job."

A final, fatal click at the other end of the line told Emery the conversation had come to an end. And so, possibly, had her career.

Mia could do more than just fire her. With her considerable influence in the industry, she could make it very tough to find another job. Emery's stomach sank. Her insides felt suddenly queasy. She had nothing without her work. She *was* nothing without it.

But at the moment there was less than nothing she could do about it. Except maybe take some time off, explore the countryside again, while she waited and hoped for a miracle.

Two days later she found herself searching for a parking spot in downtown Nashville, marveling at how little the quaint tourist town had changed. The shops along Main and Van Buren streets were as fascinating as ever, overflowing with local bounty, from homemade baskets to fresh-roasted nuts and pumpkin seeds, from gold-and-red bushels of orchard-ripened apples to gleaming glass and metal sculptures by resident artists. And woven through it all, along the roofs and rafters of the stores and restaurants, decorating nearly every well-kept cottage doorway, were the drying wreaths and vines of bittersweet, their yellow berries bursting into rays of red and orange.

Bittersweet. It was an appropriate symbol to mark her homecoming, however temporary her visit might be. The sight of the familiar country vine brought a lump to Emery's throat, reviving happy childhood memories she'd long since forgotten.

The smell of sweet baking apples that had floated from her mother's kitchen, heavy with thick, warm cream, redolent of cinnamon spices. The colorful bunches of Indian corn her father had hung from the back porch each year, decorating the house for the holidays to come. She'd missed those moments in the years away, regretted not having a family of her own to share them with. She hadn't realized how much until now.

Parking the car on a corner near the old-fashioned candy store, she stepped outside into the sweater-cool air. The scent of oven-fresh walnut fudge seduced her almost immediately. A large dose of chocolate was definitely in order here. There was no better cure for her current case of the blues.

She ducked inside, purchased a small white bag of the dark, sweet stuff, then strolled down the shop-lined street, munching along the way. Sinfully delicious, that's what it was, and possibly the last luxury she'd be able to afford for a very long time.

If she didn't bring back the diamond, and Mia fired her for it, she'd probably have to give up food for a few years. Optimistically, she rationalized that not eating for a while wouldn't be *that* bad. Besides saving money, it might be the only way she'd ever lose those extra few pounds.

Window shopping wasn't so awful either, especially when each interesting store display looked more tantalizing than the last. Stacked jars of homemade apple butter, baked goods galore, pine-needle brooms, and long strings of red licorice were only a small sampling of the local items that caught her eye. But just when she was starting to congratulate herself for passing up so many temptations, an even bigger one tapped her on the shoulder.

She spun around, startled, almost asphyxiating on her last piece of fudge. Drake! What was *he* doing here?

"Sorry, pet," he said, slapping her obligingly across the back. "I didn't mean to choke you."

"Sure," she responded with difficulty, in between several short coughing bouts. "You didn't mean for me to be attacked by bats, either, or run into a tree, or get bucked off your horse and develop bruises in the most inconvenient places you can imagine. But they all happened, didn't they?"

He didn't answer immediately. He was too busy looking down at her, smiling curiously, with a look of sincere, solemn amusement in his amazing green eyes. Emery stared back, suddenly suspicious. What new tortures did he have in mind for her now? she wondered. And what business did he have smiling at her that way? God, but he was gorgeous. It really wasn't fair for him to look so good. How was a woman supposed to maintain any sort of disinterested dignity around a man like that? Of course, being interested in him really didn't help matters much.

"Well?" she prompted.

"Well, Tasha told me I'd find you here. We need to talk."

Drake wanted to talk? That was a new one on her, Emery decided. Conversation wasn't what he'd had in mind the last time they were together. Come to think of it, she hadn't felt too much like shooting the breeze herself. But they'd both had a few days to recover from their previous encounter. Maybe a little sane, seminormal talking was exactly what they both needed right now. Preferably in a nice, safe, very public setting.

"All right," she agreed. "Where do you suggest?"

"I know just the place," he told her. Without waiting for her response, he hooked a hand under her arm and led her down a secluded side street, stopping outside a tiny storefront shack Emery'd never noticed before.

The little building itself was assembled from three-quarter logs, brown and rough-hewn, some with the bark still attached. A hand-painted sign was tacked near the front door, slightly askew. HERBAL TEAS. SPICES OUR SPECIALTY. FORTUNES TOLD.

"In here," he said, opening the door for her. "It's quiet. We can sit, have a drink."

Thirsty from the fudge, drawn by the friendly, rustic feel of the shop, Emery stepped inside. Filtered sunlight and a vague sense of claustrophobia formed her first impression.

Dried herbs and flowers were everywhere, in baskets and barrels, canisters and buckets, hanging from the ceiling in huge, feathery bunches, filling every available inch of space. A burlap sack of birdseed stood in the near corner, spilling its bounty on to the hay-strewn dirt floor as a pair of industrious brown sparrows hopped in and out of an open window, helping themselves. Row upon row of clear glass apothecary jars filled with a myriad of different spices lined the wide wooden shelves. Sassafras, arrowroot, mugwort, and frangipani were just a few of the names Emery vaguely recognized from the labels. Others were elusive, their contents unfamiliar.

Just when she was about to ask where they were expected to sit, a stocky, silver-haired woman bustled out of the back room. She wore bulky work boots beneath a full gathered dress of floral homespun. A linen apron, tied neatly around her waist, added to the no-nonsense picture she made. But a second glance revealed a fuzzy brown squirrel perched upon her shoulder, chattering noisily.

Before Emery had a chance to recover from her surprise, the woman stepped forward, reacting to the man beside her almost immediately.

"Drake!" she exclaimed enthusiastically, first

shaking his hand, then giving the effort up as not good enough and launching herself against his chest for a huge, heartfelt hug. "Good to see ya. Good to see ya!" she continued, pulling back.

The squirrel on her shoulder perked its head up at all the excitement, tail twitching, the tiny arms and legs fussing back and forth. "Come for your usual poison, have ya?" the woman asked Drake. Then her eyes narrowed inquiringly at Emery. "Who's this little bit of a thing you've brought along?"

Enduring the enthusiastic greeting with remarkable patience, Drake shot the odd woman a friendly, familiar grin. "Another old friend of mine," he said, nodding briefly at Emery. "Ms. Emery Brooks. Stubborn as you, Electra. You're going to like her."

Emery received another long, appraising glance from the strange shop owner. "Indeed?" she asked doubtfully. "Well, if you say so. Come into the back, then, you two, and I'll mix up a batch o' brew that'll make your hair stand up straight."

A batch of brew? Emery wasn't sure she liked the sound of it. What did this weird little woman keep in her back room, anyway? A cauldron full of lizard tails most likely. And how did she and Drake know each other so well? Curiosity overrode caution. She let herself be coaxed into the back and seated across from Drake at a rickety wooden table for two.

Electra retrieved a blue enamel pitcher from a nearby hutch and disappeared with it onto the rear porch.

Drake leaned back in his small wooden chair, balancing precariously on two of its narrow, carved legs. Looking perfectly at home and entirely out of place in the minuscule, mysterious setting, he shot her a wicked, satisfied wink. "Don't say I never take you anywhere."

Emery smiled in spite of herself. "Only to the finest places," she responded wryly. "What sort of shop is this, anyway? Those spices out there aren't all for cooking. Martha Stewart herself probably couldn't name half of them. And please tell me that squirrel is a pet, not part of the lunch menu."

"Fussbudget?" he asked, half grinning. "Don't worry, he's been hanging around here for years. And Electra's not exactly a cook. She's an herbalist. The plants she stocks have many uses. Medicinal, culinary. Ritualistic."

"Ritualistic? As in spells and séances, you mean. As in sacrifices. That's it, isn't it? She's a witch and I'm about to become your latest burnt offering."

A sensual smile melted the wintergreen eyes to warm, sizzling fields of summer. "Sorry, Em, but I believe a ceremony of that nature would require a virgin. And we both know you can consider yourself safe on that score. Very safe, from what I remember."

She drew in a quick breath, her face growing hot from his words. Did he have to remind her? It wasn't as if she could ever forget.

He was right, of course. Naturally, she was no virgin. He'd seen to that in the most thorough way imaginable. Actually, in several of the most thorough ways. But if she had that night to live over again, she wouldn't want it to be any different. She still would have done exactly the same thing. God help her, but she wished she *did* have that night to live over again.

"Never mind that," she told him, dismissing a subject that was far too dangerous to broach again. "We do need to talk, Drake. We were good at that, once, among other things. I just hope we can still remember how."

Electra ducked back inside the small room, bearing the bright blue pitcher again. A caramel-tinted liquid leaked in tiny, moist droplets from its narrow spout.

"This stuff'll make ya talk," she promised with a delighted laugh, pouring out two tumblers of the drink, unapologetic for her apparent eavesdropping.

To Emery's surprise, Drake didn't seem to mind the woman's interference. He gave her a tolerant smile instead, and solemnly thanked her, taking a long, grateful swallow from the glass she'd handed him. Emery stared hesitantly at hers, wondering if she should follow suit. What was in there, anyway?

It did smell sweet. Dark, strong, and full of fragrant spices. And she *was* very thirsty. Witch's brew or not, she didn't care. She hoped it would make her feel strange. She hoped it would make her wild and euphoric. Or at least give her the courage to face Drake Tallen on his own terms. Just this once. She picked up the glass and drank.

SIX

Emery's eyes widened in surprise as Electra's pungent brew worked its way down her throat. "Easy," Drake warned her. "That's the strongest sun-brewed tea this side of St. Louis."

"Tea?" she asked him, incredulous, almost disappointed that it wasn't some crazy magic concoction she'd been sipping after all. What had she been hoping for, anyway? A love potion? An aphrodisiac? Something that would cause her to throw good sense to the wind, remove every last one of her carefully guarded inhibitions? "Is that all it is?"

Electra's small shoulders rose in indignation. Her voice grew huffy. "Is that *all?* I'll have you know, girlie, that recipe took me thirty years to perfect. And you'd better watch out. It packs a powerful punch."

"I'm sure it does," Emery agreed diplomatically.

"I just thought—I'm sorry. I don't know what I thought. It is delicious."

Drake watched Electra warming to the compliment, nodding her approval. He smiled to himself. Em always had been resourceful. Never more so than when she was cornered. He'd like nothing more than to crowd her now, forget all about their little talk, and entice her to change her mind about the deal. But that wasn't why he'd brought her here today.

He waited for the older woman to bustle off again before he spoke. What he had to say to Em was personal, too private to share. Besides the fact he'd prefer not to make an idiot of himself in front of Electra. Her friendship and respect had meant a lot to him over the years, and he didn't want to risk it by revealing what a soft, sentimental fool he really was.

"You win," he said quietly, meeting Emery's astounded glance across the table. "I'm ready to sell to Swank's," he told her. "For cash, that is, if your offer still stands."

Her look of surprise brought him little satisfaction. Had she imagined he was incapable of compromise or compassion? Would she ever find it in her heart to forgive him for what he'd done to her ten years ago? Hell, how could he expect to find absolution from Emery when he was incapable of forgiving himself?

Hurting her had been bad enough. But his greatest sin went far beyond that. He'd been too damn proud and defensive back then for his own good. Or anyone else's.

It was that idiotic, infernal pride of his that had made him want to win Tasha, take over the quarry, prove to the whole town that he wasn't just some low-life piece of trash that his parents had dumped and left behind. But it was his pride that had ended up wounding the people he admired the most. The people who'd been there with him when times were bad. His grandfather. Emery.

And no matter how much money he'd made in the meantime, no matter what a big man he'd become with the locals, or how many diamonds he was willing to sacrifice for her sake, his own redemption still remained just beyond his reach.

"Actually," Emery told him, her eyes still wide with wonder, "I've been authorized to up the amount by another ten thousand."

"Fine," he agreed, feeling nothing. The settlement figures should've had some effect on him. They didn't. He hadn't been holding out for more money. He'd been holding on to a lucky talisman, hoping it might save him somehow, make up for all the old mistakes.

But there were some things he'd done that could never be mended. And saving her was the only thing that mattered at the moment.

She blinked at him in confusion, still in a state of apparent shock. "Fine?" she repeated, looking more flustered than ever. "Whoa. Back up a second, buster, because I don't get it. What made you change your mind?"

"Let's just say I had a revelation about the solution to our little problem."

She studied him carefully, her eyes full of the same intense curiosity that had always fascinated him. "I don't believe it," she protested. "Since when do you change your mind so easily?"

He shot her a slow, thoughtful smile. "I promise you, Em, it wasn't easy."

But she was unwilling to let the issue drop, in spite of the fact that she'd finally gotten her way. "I still don't understand," she pressed him. "Why the sudden about-face? What's happened since the last time we talked?"

He lifted his eyebrows, amused at her characteristic reaction. So, winning wasn't all that mattered to her. She wanted to play fair, did she? She wanted some honesty. Well, he was willing to give her that as well. He only hoped they were both ready to handle it.

"Disappointed, Em?" he asked her quietly. "Sure you wouldn't rather have been the one to change your mind?"

"No. Certainly not. Of course not."

He downed the dregs of Electra's brew and planted his tumbler on the table. "Maybe you're just afraid I figured it out."

She waited a few seconds before asking the next, most obvious question. Was it fear that made her hesitate, he wondered, or hope? "Figured what out?"

"That you're really not worth a fortune."

She exhaled slowly, as if the impact of his words had struck her with physical force. "I—I *know* I'm not."

The catch in her voice made his gut ache. Hell, he hated to hurt her like that. But she really believed she wasn't worth it, partly because of him. She was so bloody sure of her own faults, she couldn't risk seeing herself any other way. He'd wanted to shock her to insight. How else could he make her listen?

"You may believe that, pet. I never will. Don't you see you're priceless? In spite of the flaws. No, *because* of them. Just remember that, when you're back in Chicago, checking out some inanimate stone. Those rocks you admire so much are worthless, no matter how perfect. They might be lovely to look at, or last for all eternity, but none of that matters. *Life* is more fragile, more ephemeral, more important. More valuable. Don't underestimate the cost of yours."

Soft pools of tears collected at the corners of her eyes. "Why are you telling me this?"

"Because you need to hear it, Em. Because I owe you that much for forcing you back here, disrupting your life." And disrupting his.

"Why did you change your mind again about selling the stone?"

Drake hesitated. Why? Because he'd been completely blown away by how stubborn, sexy, and sweetly unsure of herself she was. Because he'd developed a definite weakness for a pair of wide, vulnerable brown eyes.

"Tasha called me," he finally explained. "Told me your boss is giving you a pretty bad time over all this."

"So it's pity, then," she said, still fighting tears. "You feel sorry for me."

It was all Drake could do to keep from knocking away the table between them and gathering her into his arms again. How much he wanted to comfort her at this moment, to help her ease the pain in physical pleasure. He spoke to her instead, his voice coarse with desire, heavy with heat. "I'm sorry for both of us, Em. But I won't be responsible for you losing your job. It means a lot to you, doesn't it?"

Emery nodded, wondering how to make Drake understand just how important her work had become to her. "Sometimes I think I should thank you for not wanting to marry me back then. I was so young, I had no idea who I was at seventeen, what kinds of things I might be good at. Tasha was the one who'd always gotten the attention. But when I was forced out on my own, I discovered I could be strong, self-sufficient, smart. I made a career for myself, found what I was best at. Not being beautiful, but evaluating beautiful things. The people at Swank's know I have an eye for it, a certain skill. I've earned my place there. It would hurt to lose it."

"So you won't have to now," he said.

"No," she agreed. "Thanks to you." He'd saved

her from that. Saved her job, her identity, restored everything that mattered to her by agreeing to sell Swank's the stone. She blinked the tears from her eyes, swallowing hard. "Drake, I—I'm so grateful."

"Don't be," he told her. "I don't want your gratitude."

"Then what do you want?" she asked him softly.

He reached across the table to wipe a stray drop of moisture from her face. "Your forgiveness," he said. "Which may be a lot more than I deserve."

Emery's breath caught when his fingers made contact with her skin. Sudden, unexpected, sensual contact. She felt the sweet shock of his touch racing all the way down to her toes. An urgent sigh slipped from her throat.

Drake's eyes flared at the sound, flashing green fire her way. "Don't." He dropped his hand to the table again, catching her by the wrist before she had the opportunity to touch him back. "Look at me like that again and you're only tempting fate. Take my advice now, Ms. Brooks. Draw up a purchase order. Write me a check. Do whatever you have to, but take the diamond and run."

Tempting fate? Yes, she supposed that *was* what she'd been doing. Tempting *him*. But for some inexplicable reason, she couldn't bring herself to stop. She didn't pull her wrist away. Instead, she wrapped her small hand around his larger one. "It's not that simple," she explained. "It'll take a couple of days minimum before Swank's will send the money. I couldn't leave town now, even if I wanted to."

She felt Drake's muscles tense beneath her touch. "Are you saying you don't want to leave?"

"Not immediately," she said. "Not yet. I was hoping to stick around for a bit. Play tourist, at least for this afternoon." She drew in a deep breath. "Why don't we spend a few hours together, for old times' sake? Hang around the way we used to. As friends."

"Friends?" he repeated doubtfully, his eyebrows lifting. "Don't fool yourself, Em. Friends don't kiss the way we did just a few days ago. I don't want to be your buddy."

"You were," she said wistfully. "Once."

"No," he said, slowly grinning. "You hounded me mercilessly until I had to let you hang around. There was no getting rid of you. You were a pest."

"I was not!"

"You wanted me bad, babe. Wouldn't leave me alone."

"What? You wish."

Fussbudget protested loudly from the other room, adding his two cents to the heated conversation. Electra puttered back in shortly afterward. "Now, then," she asked calmly. "Anyone ready for more tea?"

"Better cut her off," Drake suggested with a cocky smile, nodding toward Emery. "One shot of the brew and her memory's going already."

No, Emery reasoned. Her mind was totally intact. It was her heart that had started melting to warm slush the minute she'd seen him smile again.

She'd forgotten what it was like, that boyish, defiant grin of his that could radiate the corners of the darkest room. No woman was safe from it. Not grandmothers. Not great-grandmothers.

Not even Electra.

A dollop of tea sloshed out of the pitcher she was holding. "I'd say it's having near as much effect on you," the older woman said, staring at Drake. "Five years you've been coming here, and never a look like that." She shot a curious glance at Emery, half-suspicious, half-respectful. "Is this your doing, girlie? Have you set him under some kind of spell?"

"I—no, of course not," she answered solemnly. "I wouldn't know how."

"You sure about that?" Electra asked. "I noticed something fuzzy around you, hon, the minute you walked into my shop. A glow, I'd call it. You're not trying to fool ol' Electra now, are you? I'm a hard one to hide things from."

Emery didn't doubt it. The woman had the instincts of a psychic, it seemed. A glow? The accuracy of it sent shivers down her spine. Was it the curse that was causing the aura around her? she wondered. Or was it something else?

"I promise, I have nothing to hide," she insisted, maybe a little too forcefully. Just who was it she wanted to convince?

"Don't mind then, do you, if I read your fortune?"

Emery glanced at Drake, a question in her eyes.

"Go ahead," he assured her. "You wanted to play

tourist. This is as good a place as any to start. Electra's one of Nashville's most popular attractions. Pretty accurate too."

The older woman flushed with pleasure at the praise. "Now, then. Nothing much to mixing up a few spices, reading some tea leaves here and there." She turned again to Emery. "But I *did* predict the great snowstorm of sixty-five, as well as the birth of Mrs. Wakefield's triplets. Hand me your glass, then, honey, and let's see what the future has in store for you."

Emery obeyed, watching in fascination as Electra stared, trancelike, at the bottom of her tumbler. Tiny bits of tea leaves and a smattering of spices had collected there, forming some mysterious pattern that only a fortune-teller could decipher. Fuss-budget went suddenly still on her shoulder, seeming to understand the quiet concentration his mistress required. Even the birds outside grew silent as a slow, sweet humming sounded from the bottom of Electra's throat.

Humming? Emery felt the hair on the back of her neck stand on end. Something was happening to the older woman as she tried to decode the hidden message. Something strange.

"I see clouds," she said, her voice low and melodic. "Shadows, everywhere. Your soul in hiding."

"My . . . soul?"

"I see fear. Daylight breaking at the end of a long, passionate night. A man is with you. A man you love."

"Oh," Emery whispered, afraid to ask who it was. Afraid of the answer she already knew.

"You have something for him. A gift? No, a surprise. Something unexpected. Seductive."

"Oh."

"I see—" Her voice broke off as she looked up, startled, glancing from Emery to Drake and back again. "There is a cloud around you," she said, coming slowly out of the trance. "I can see no more."

Emery wondered what it was Electra had been about to say, what it was that had surprised her speechless. The curse? Was something else going to happen to her? But the fortune-teller's vision hadn't seemed at all connected to the diamond.

"You didn't happen to notice anything small and green in there anywhere, did you? A little rock maybe, that has a strange habit of sometimes turning red?"

"The Devil's Diamond?" Electra asked, a light of understanding dawning in her clear gray eyes. "Yes, that might account for the fuzzy emanations I've been getting. Not to worry, honey," she added, patting Emery sympathetically on the head. "We'll get a better reading next time. Come back and see me when the spell on the stone is broken."

"When the—you know about the curse, then?"

"Naturally. It's common knowledge around these parts."

"Any ideas how to go about breaking it?" It seemed everyone understood the diamond's inner mysteries except her. But then, it wasn't a subject her gemology training had prepared her for. Removing Hexes 101. Too bad there hadn't been a course like that in her curriculum.

"That's an easy one, girlie," Electra confessed. "The stone must be cut."

Cut? Well, of course, that was impossible. The diamond didn't belong to her. And sawing it in half would likely lessen the value. A lot.

"Isn't there any other way to protect myself from it?" she asked hopefully.

Drake, who had been perfectly silent, finally offered a suggestion. "Only one," he responded in answer to her question. "You can be very nice to its owner."

Electra let out a long, appreciative laugh. "Diabolus!" she said, shaking her head. "He is wise, like the dragon."

"A wise guy is more like it," Emery muttered.

"Isn't it his turn now?" she asked, pointing to Drake's empty glass. "I'd just love to hear what's lurking in *that* pile of tea leaves."

"Impossible," Electra explained. "He is unreadable."

"Yes," Emery agreed. "I've noticed that."

He laughed, taking her by the arm. "Come on," he urged. "We've taken up enough of Electra's time. If you're still up for some sightseeing, I'll give you a lift."

Emery didn't miss the warm handshake that passed between Drake and the slightly eccentric fortune-teller. After adding her own thanks for Electra's hospitality, she waved good-bye and stepped outside into the cooling autumn air.

"You're good friends with her, aren't you?" she asked Drake, shooting him a speculative glance.

"She used to work for me," he responded. "But she went through some hard times when her husband died. Lost her house. So I gave her my old cottage and helped set her up in her own business. She's a tough lady. Likes to do things her own way. I respect that about her."

Emery felt a fleeting pang of envy. Drake's respect was a hard thing to earn. It meant something. His admiration wasn't based on age, or looks, or even the appearance of success. He had a way of looking beyond all that and seeing inside a person's mind. Inside their heart.

"You *gave* her your old house?" she repeated.

"Sure," he acknowledged. "It wasn't much, I know, but I had it fixed up a little. At least it was a place to live."

"Sounds pretty generous to me. So where were you living at the time?"

"I'd just bought my acreage," he explained. "I camped out there for a while. Moved into the cavern for shelter one rainy day and decided it was a pretty good spot to settle down in."

A black Jeep convertible, complete with rollbars and turbochargers, was parked at the curb. Drake strode toward it.

"Yours?" she asked, surprised. But somehow, the machine suited him. Like a sleek, preening hawk, poised on the road, ready to fly. "Very high-tech for a Cro-Magnon cave-dweller. I thought you were more comfortable riding bareback."

He shrugged. "I'm adaptive. Besides, Stealth can only do thirty miles an hour, tops. This beauty could hit a hundred if I asked her to. And she's still one hundred percent horsepower." He swung himself deftly into the driver's seat. "Ready to roll?"

Emery hesitated. "In a second," she told him. "But I have something to say to you first."

"What's that, pet?" he asked, glancing over at her.

"I do forgive you," she told him, "for everything."

He reached up and tilted her face toward him until their eyes were perfectly aligned. "Why, Em?" he asked, searching her expression.

"Because I see now, it would never have worked out."

"Oh?"

"No," she insisted. "Marriage was never the answer for us."

He hesitated before answering. "Probably not."

"And it wouldn't work now," she added. "I can't stay."

There was another brief pause. "I can't ask you to."

Emery assured herself it was relief she felt instead of disappointment. "I just want you to understand that this time no promises are necessary."

"This time?"

"No complications," she continued, drawing in a deep breath, looking him straight in those deep, quicksand eyes. "Except one," she admitted softly.

"Which one is that, Em?"

"I still want to sleep with you."

SEVEN

"So then you asked him for a date?" Tasha repeated. "Emery, I don't know how you had the nerve!"

Emery still wasn't completely sure where she'd found the courage herself. And Tasha didn't know the half of it. She believed the date her innocent little sister had made with Drake was for the Autumn Ball only. She didn't know the original offer had been for her to spend the night as well.

Thank goodness she didn't know. It would've been bad enough to admit she'd practically begged Drake Tallen to take her to bed. Even more humiliating was the fact that he'd turned her down.

So far. He *had* agreed to attend the ball with her, after recovering from his temporary shock. But he'd refused to commit to anything more.

Why?

She'd assured him there were no strings attached this time. No father to forbid whatever happened between two consenting adults. No vows to make. None to break.

But that was exactly what had seemed to bother him. The sex without strings. The sin without ceremony.

Very weird, since he'd been willing to swap the same thing for the stone just a few days ago. What was it, she wondered, that had made him change his mind? And how was she going to change it back again?

She needed that night with him, now more than ever. It was the sacrifice he'd made that had finally settled it in her mind. Drake's agreeing to sell the gem to save her job.

She wanted to give him something special in return, to show him her forgiveness was for real. To help him forgive himself. Because she was starting to understand that he might need that one night together even more than she did.

Sleeping with Drake would heal both of their wounds at once. It would give them closure in the most intimate way imaginable and let them finally move on with their lives.

But it was going to take some convincing to get Drake to go along with her plan. A slow seduction, that's what she had in mind. A temptation to overcome his every objection.

An enticement that would begin with the perfect dress.

"I need your help, Tasha." She scanned the back room of the bridal shop, unsure of just where to start. There were so many outfits to choose from! Gowns of every conceivable style and color. Dressing for work, she could handle. Professional, conservative clothes were easy to mix and match. But dressing up was something she'd never been good at.

"What do people wear to balls these days, anyway?" she asked. "I mean, it isn't really a ball, right? It's just a dance. And a local dance at that. I wouldn't want to be overdressed. Maybe something plain and simple . . ."

"No way," Tasha told her, taking charge. "Simple is out, Em. I say you should go for spectacular and gaudy. Lots of beads, plenty of leg showing. Bosom too. We'll start in the strapless section."

"*Bosom?*" Emery asked, alarmed. "Do I even have one? And if I do, do I really want to *show* it?"

"Sure you do, sister. You'll see."

Emery groaned. "Omigod, that's what I'm afraid of. If I go strapless, everyone else is going to see too."

"Of course," Tasha agreed calmly. "That's the point, isn't it? What's the use in dressing up if you can't have a little fun doing it?"

"Fun? Fun, ha! Fun for you, maybe, Ms. Flawless Body. You're used to people staring at your bosom. A perfect one, I might add. I'm not!"

"You're joking, right? Perfect? Oh, Em, I've never told anybody this, but I think one of my breasts is higher than the other. Look!" She turned sideways in front of the mirror and lifted her blouse.

"Fifty bucks for this bra and I swear they're still out of proportion."

They glanced in the mirror, then back at each other. Both of them burst out laughing.

Emery sank down onto the love seat, still giggling and slightly stunned. "I can't believe you think there's something wrong with you. I've never admitted this to you before, either, Tasha, but I've always been jealous of you. Not just because of how pretty you are, but mostly because of Drake."

"You still love him, don't you?" her sister asked.

"I—I'm not sure. I *think* it's love, but it's a little hard to separate from the schoolgirl crush I always had on him. Anyway, I'm trying to find out."

"Well, I'm sure," Tasha told her. "And I think he feels the same way about you. He just doesn't know it yet."

"Oh, right," Emery responded in disbelief. "And the next thing you'll be telling me is that you're going to play fairy godmother and get the two of us together."

"Well, I did phone Drake about the trouble you were in over the stone, didn't I?"

"Yes," Emery admitted. "You did. That was nice of you, Tasha."

"Well, I have my moments. Besides, I feel pretty bad about everything that's happened between the three of us. And I think it would be pretty great if the two of you ended up together, after all. Now, what are we going to do about that dress—"

Tasha's big blue eyes gleamed as she spied a particularly low-cut confection on the nearest, glittering rack. "That's *it*," she said solemnly, seizing the sexiest, skimpiest, most stunning sequined gown by the hanger and holding it up for closer inspection. "It's perfect with your hair."

Emery braced herself. She couldn't wear anything close to that. It was too beautiful for her. Too dangerously daring. Too downright *small*. "That's not a dress," she protested. "It's a bathing suit."

"Silly, it's divine. Here, try it on."

Emery shot the slender, beaded ribbon of slinky fabric a doubtful look. "How? With a shoehorn?"

"Nonsense," Tasha persisted. "Now scoot on into the dressing room and slip it over that hard head of yours. It's going to look smashing."

"More likely I'm going to look smashed into it."

"*Go*," Tasha commanded. "And quit arguing. Honestly, Emery, if I didn't know better I'd say you were scared to look your best."

That did it. The sisterly challenge was irresistible. "I am not scared. Hand it over."

Five minutes later she emerged from the dressing room. Slowly. Her hands were over her face.

"Still afraid?" Tasha teased. "Don't be. Just look in the mirror. It's *you*."

Cautiously, Emery turned to face her worst critic. That sick, sadistic length of silvered glass. The mirror. Herself. They were one and the same.

She parted her hands, peering through the wedge-shaped windows of space between her fingers. And saw the most amazing thing.

Someone pretty. A person completely unique. Wearing a dress to die for.

To say the gown was lovely, or elegant, or dramatic, simply didn't do it justice. It was *voluptuous*.

It plunged. It plummeted. It was bold and baring, shimmering with soft metallic highlights that seemed to set her hair on fire. And yes, she *did* have a bosom. The dress made that perfectly clear. It even bulged in all the right spots.

It definitely wasn't her.

Thank goodness.

She turned toward Tasha. "What do you think?"

Her sister smiled with satisfaction. "I think our old flame is in for some serious trouble."

Drake Tallen knew all about trouble. Avoiding it was never what he'd been best at. Facing it was more his style, owning up to the mistakes he'd made, the rules he'd broken, especially in his younger days. Learning to meditate had helped him do that.

But the problem he was facing tonight called for some stronger medicine. A tall shot of rye whiskey and a raw, rancid, hand-rolled cigar. Sometimes the demons had to be sent smoking, or numbed by a highball or two. On dark nights like this one, there was a lot to be said for the more primitive forms of meditation. Fire and firewater. Good weapons because they worked.

The wet bar in his dining room was slate-topped, polished smooth, and stacked full of crystal decanters. He poured himself a generous drink, letting the liquid rise to the uppermost edges of the sharply cut glass. The stogie came next. He bit the end off with his teeth, struck a match on the countertop, and flared the tip with flame. Inhaling deeply, he thought of her.

Mind control, that's what was called for in the tough case of Emery Brooks. The strength of the spirit over the flesh. The brain over the body.

The balance was delicate, like walking a narrow branch across a deep canyon gorge. One slip and you were history. One trip and every rule a man tried to live by went suddenly over the edge.

She had made him stumble with her sensual suggestion. She'd left him thunderstruck. One sentence from her sweet, willing mouth, and his karma was completely out of control. Shot straight to hell and back by the idea of her wanting to sleep with him.

He slid into a wing chair, tilted his head back, and blew slow curls of smoke toward the cavern ceiling. What the devil had he done?

His proposal had been a ploy. He'd never imagined she would take him up on it, not in his wildest dreams. But, apparently, that's exactly what his pet had in mind.

Fulfilling his wildest dreams.

She was offering him a gift far greater than the one he'd given her. Just the idea of her tenderness toward him rocked him straight to his soul. No one in his life had ever shown him the kind of sexy, unselfish sweetness that this woman did. No one else had ever cared enough to bother.

But he couldn't risk making love with Emery again. He couldn't allow himself to accept the physical gratification she was ready to bestow because there were too many emotions involved this time. Hers. His. Hell, they were both beyond the point of the casual sex she'd suggested.

He wasn't sure he could make love to her again and let her go for good. But, of course, that's what would have to happen if they were going to have that night. And the last thing he wanted between him and Em was another messy good-bye. The last thing he wanted was for anyone to end up getting hurt.

But rejecting the amazing offer she'd made him seemed almost as impossible. Em was just beginning to believe in herself, just starting to realize what a sensual, irresistible woman she was. If he did decide to resist her now, what was it going to do to her fragile, newly forming self-esteem?

Who was he kidding? What was resisting her going to do to him?

His own motivations were hardly altruistic. He wouldn't have to make believe how much he wanted her, just to boost her ego. Because he did want her.

He had since the moment she'd returned to town. But she'd made it more than clear how much her job in Chicago meant to her. And he wasn't about to propose anything permanent to a woman who would only be running away from him again.

Marriage, of course, was out of the question. Being left at the altar once in a lifetime was enough for any man.

But a date was all he'd promised her. An escort to the Autumn Ball. Surely he could get through one innocent evening without any major complications. He'd managed to live without Emery Brooks for the past ten years. How hard could it be to keep his hands off her for a single, innocuous night?

Drake took the curve into Tasha's driveway, wheeling the Jeep to a stop in front of the old Brooks house. From the little he'd seen of it a decade ago, it was still pretty much as he remembered. Ordinary. Nice. Right out of a 1950s picture postcard, the kind with the whole family sitting on the front porch wearing their Sunday best, smiling. The kind of home he'd never had.

He'd wanted it once, the dream, but not any longer. A man could only believe in fantasies like that for so long.

Tonight he'd actually been invited inside the hallowed sanctuary, an honor that had rarely been offered him before. Bad-boy troublemakers from broken homes weren't usually welcome in middle-class living rooms. Not unless there were details to discuss for an impending shotgun wedding. Tonight, he promised himself, would hold no such problems.

A date, that's all this was. An annual networking opportunity he usually attended for the sake of business. Friendly business. This evening would be no different.

They'd have a couple of drinks, spin around the room for a number or two, and it would all be over. He'd deliver the diamond, kiss her on the forehead, and send her back to Chicago where she belonged. It would be easy, done with, and she would be behind him.

At least that's what he believed until the minute she opened the door.

Just breathing was hard from the second he saw her in that dress. She looked dynamite. Drop-dead, stop-a-clock sexy. Even better than she had in her filmy white wedding gown.

Hotter. Sweeter. With a look of such provocative invitation on her face, he knew almost immediately what she had on her mind, the enticing little flirt.

Seduction.

Aw, hell, but he was in trouble. Because he was determined she wasn't going to get her way. Not this time.

"Emery. Going to invite me in?"

"Please," she said politely, stepping aside to let him pass.

Drake glanced briefly around the formal living room, deciding it was pretty close to what he'd expected of Tasha's taste. Serene, slightly stuffy, and perfectly symmetrical, right down to the matched sets of leather-bound books flanking either side of the fireplace shelves. Everything neat and uncluttered. Everything in its proper place. Dull and impeccable. A pretty good picture of what his life would've been like with her.

There was no sign of Tasha or her husband, though. Milton must've known he was coming. And Tasha's business usually kept her from attending the fall dance herself. She was still at her shop, no doubt, seeing to the last-minute needs of her fashion-conscious customers.

Which meant he and Emery were alone. So maybe sticking around to see the rest of the place wasn't such a good idea. With no sister nearby to chaperon, there was no telling what would happen.

Come to think of it, yes there was. Wild, wanton, abandoned lovemaking. He couldn't even *look* at her without thinking about it.

"Shouldn't you grab a sweater or something?" he suggested. An overcoat. Some sweatpants. Anything opaque would help. Anything with real fabric.

What was that outfit made of anyway? A few sequins? A little elastic? Whoever had designed it was obviously a sadistic imbecile. Didn't they realize a woman could die of hypothermia going out in the elements wearing nothing but glitter? Didn't they realize a man would have to wrap his arms around her the whole evening, just to keep her warm?

Whoever had designed it was obviously a genius.

"I'll be fine," she told him. "The auditorium's heated. So is your car, right?"

"Right," he agreed, holding out his arm. But it was going to be overheated as soon as she stepped into it. He could feel the warm beads of sweat breaking out on his forehead already. "Em," he said quietly. "You look—great."

But he knew it was an understatement. A blatant bold-faced lie. And he was ashamed of himself for it. If she'd been brave enough to wear that dress, woman enough, which she clearly was, he ought to be man enough to admit it. He just didn't want to be man enough to do anything else about it.

"No," he said, correcting himself. "You look spectacular."

Her eyes lit up at the compliment, making Drake swear hotly under his breath. Damn, but she was so sexy when she smiled. It was the tight little tilt of her chin that really got him, the enigmatic expression on her face. The woman was willful, stubborn, a spark against flint.

She didn't have a clue what she did to him. One look, one innocent smile, and his insides flared, banking below to a slow, sinful burn. At least he had a pretty good clue what he wanted to do to her.

Nothing, he reminded himself vehemently. Survival was the only goal on his evening agenda. Simple, instinctive survival.

"Thanks," she said sincerely. "I was just thinking the same thing about you. Black is definitely your color."

A sigh welled inside Emery as she uttered the words. Actually, Drake looked good in everything, but the tuxedo he wore tonight was the ultimate in masculine elegance. Black sapphire shirt studs flashed against the brilliance of his starched white dress shirt.

The silk of his bow tie, expertly arranged, snaked around his neck in a single satin ribbon, flaring to sharp wings at the center of his throat. He was a dream in light and dark. A handsome, haunting phantasm of sleek male perfection. Drake Tallen, the devil in black, at his most dashing.

Better yet, he seemed to like what she was wearing. His icy-hot eyes had taken in every inch of her dress, glinting with undisguised approval. But it wasn't only the outfit he seemed to be interested in.

His glance at her hair hinted that the idea of touching it was foremost in his mind. The tension in his mouth as he took in the bare stretches of her skin told her kissing was also in his thoughts. The tight curl of his lips showed how much he wanted to taste her, the iridescence in his eyes showed her where.

She blinked hard for a second, praying it was real, hoping that it wasn't wishful thinking. Her plan was starting to work. She'd caught his interest with the gown. Now if she could only keep her nerve to continue.

She retrieved her purse and shawl, linking her arm in his, gratefully letting him lead her to the car. The metallic leather heels she wore were the highest she'd ever owned. Unfortunately, she hadn't had much time to get used to them. She could maneuver well enough, but no matter how carefully she walked in them, her hips seemed to sway provocatively from side to side.

They reached the passenger-side door, but Drake didn't open it immediately. He seemed to have something else on his mind. "The fresh air feels good," he said, catching her against him. "You feel good."

Good? It felt like heaven having him hold her like that, Emery decided. She wasn't the least bit cold, in spite of the chill night air. Her insides were warm and sizzling with anticipation. Her stomach was fluttering, her belly on fire. A fierce tension was mounting between them tonight, a contest of wills, a challenge that had started in the shape of a sequined dress.

She sensed his resistance, even as he held her. He knew the trap had been laid. But he was toying with the bait, debating whether or not to take a bite.

She hugged her arms across her chest, leaning against him. It didn't matter who won anymore. This was all that mattered, the here and now. She laughed softly. "I feel like a kid on her first date."

"I guess it *is* our first date," he agreed. "A little late, but at least we got around to it."

"And there's no curfew," she teased. "I don't even have to be home by midnight."

"Oh, yes you do," he responded, releasing his hold on her, helping her into the car. "Safe and sound, snug in your own little bed," he added, shutting her door with determined finality.

"With you there to tuck me in?" she asked innocently, as soon as he'd seated himself behind the wheel.

"Toss you out more likely," he told her, firing up the engine.

She crossed her legs and several shimmering yards of dress fell away, baring a long stretch of leg straight up to her thigh. She heard him groan.

She was starting to enjoy herself.

Ten minutes later they entered the auditorium, arm in arm. Several people in the packed hall signaled to Drake in greeting. His was a familiar face in this crowd of the community. He might be the kind of man who liked to do things his own way, but the civic leaders had to agree, he did them well. The rock quarry he owned and ran was one of the most thriving businesses in the area. Many solid, local jobs had resulted from his success. A number of employees who came forward to shake his hand seemed sincerely glad to see him. His competitors simply looked on in grudging respect.

Seconds later it was Emery who became the center of attention. People were curious about her, a position she definitely wasn't used to.

"Everyone's staring," she whispered to Drake.

"Naturally. They can't help themselves."

She glanced around the brightly decorated room. Dried fall foliage decked the linen-covered tables. A cornucopia of a buffet, overflowing with autumn bounty, was set up against the back wall, complete with carved pumpkins, baked-bread soup bowls, and an ice sculpture in the shape of a giant acorn squash. But all Emery could see were several hundred pairs of very interested eyes, looking back at her.

"It's—impolite," she insisted, at a loss how to handle so much unsolicited attention.

Tasha, naturally, would've known what to do. "Head up!" she'd say. "Chest out, and keep smiling even if your face falls off."

But Emery's strongest urge was to suck everything back in at the moment and crawl quietly underneath the nearest table.

Luckily, Drake's arm, planted proprietarily on her waist, stopped her short from doing that. "It's involuntary on their part," he assured her. "Believe me."

"They want to know who your date is, don't they?" she inquired hopefully, still uncomfortable at the amount of commotion their entrance had caused.

"No," he corrected, guiding her smoothly onto the dance floor and immediately into his arms. "They want to know who that gorgeous woman is and how she ended up in that bastard Tallen's evil clutches. At this very moment men all over the room are just dying to rescue you."

She blinked up at him, smiling. "You won't let them, will you?"

"The first one who speaks to you is dead meat. Pulverized, I promise."

"Hmmm . . . sounds a little rough."

"It's gonna take a little rough to keep them away

from you tonight. Hell, it's gonna take more than a little to keep *me* away."

"Why fight it, then?" She tilted her head back, flirting so outrageously she could barely believe it. She knew what she was fooling with.

Hellfire and damnation. The sinful, sexy look in Drake Tallen's eyes promised no less. No doubt about it, she was dancing with danger.

But something about the dress and the stares and the risks she'd already taken made her want to take more. Throwing caution to the wind, she realized, could be very cathartic. Let them look, she thought. Let them stare. As long as he was staring at her, too, nothing else mattered.

"Just give me a minute," he said, gathering her tightly to him, so deliciously tight she could barely breathe. "I'll think of a good reason."

But all sense of reason had already fled from Emery's mind. The feelings she had weren't rational. They were too hot to handle. She was melting against the rock wall of his chest, sinking into his massive, masculine form like some wispy, ethereal being floating through a dark, erotic dream.

The music slowed to a rhythmic pulse as the lights in the room went dim, coaxing the dancers into leisurely, insistent synchronization. Emery let her head drop against Drake's shoulder, surrendering to the soft, steady beat, surrendering to him. He was so smooth on his feet, so sure of his moves across the floor, she didn't have to think of her own. He had the grace of a panther as he swayed his lean, muscled body back and forth with hers in mirror-image motion.

"I had no idea you were so good," she murmured against the satin of his lapel.

"None?" he asked her softly, working his long, expert fingers down the length of her spine. Down, down he went, pressing her pelvis so close to his that dental floss wouldn't be able to work its way between them. "I'll take that as a compliment, my sweet, but frankly, I should be insulted."

"So good at *dancing*," she amended, her face still buried in his shoulder, grateful he wasn't able to see the expression on her face. Lord, but she knew he was good at *that*. So good she was practically flinging herself into his arms at this very moment, pleading for more. No, she'd already flung. At this point she was melting, mesmerized by the mastery of his touch.

The seduction was working, she realized. On her. Some saucy, brazen vixen she was. One stroke, one word, one single dance with Drake, and she was already putty in his hands.

"Dancing?" he asked doubtfully, tracing his other hand up the tender nape of her neck, catching a mass of her hair and drawing it toward his face, breathing in her scent. "Is that what they call this? I don't think so, pet. It's just a socially acceptable ritual to perform unspeakably illicit acts in public. Just consider for a moment. Would I be able to do this to you with everyone watching if there weren't any music?"

His hand palmed the curve of her backside with sweet, shocking familiarity, electrifying nerve endings she'd never known she had before. Emery was so stunned by the audacity of it, by the sudden longing his forbidden touch had produced inside her, she had little time to react. Before she'd even begun to get used to what his fingers were doing, he tipped her head back just far enough to take her simultaneously with his mouth. The kiss he planted on her was deep, deliberate. So thorough and earth-shattering, it nearly stripped her senseless.

She could feel the tug of his desire all the way through her, thrumming straight down until the soles of her feet were vibrantly quivering. It was similar to the sensation she'd had on his galloping horse, only sharper this time, far more exquisite. The sensation of flying, of losing control.

It stunned her that one kiss from Drake could bring her so much pleasure. Blushing, burning, resonating pleasure that stirred a chord inside her stronger than the taut, sensual strings of the music welling all around them.

Yet it was a kiss of fair warning, she realized. The message from his mouth was unmistakable.

Don't tempt me, pet, his lips said silently against hers. *I'm not in the mood for games. Don't lie down with the devil if you're afraid of the dark.*

EIGHT

Emery felt rooted to the dance floor by the shocking jolts of excitement running through her. Drunk with sensation, stunned by the sheer daring of what Drake was doing, she didn't do so much as murmur a faint protest. How could she stop him, anyway? He was larger, stronger, a sorcerer in black, mesmerizing her with his powerful, sensual magic.

Erotic enchantment, that's what it was. Irresistible, sexual spell weaving.

He released her the moment the music ended. "Let's find a table," he suggested. "I'm sure we could both use a drink."

Unfortunately, Drake realized, one-hundred-proof grain alcohol wouldn't begin to relieve what was ailing him tonight. Or Emery, he decided, noting the soft flush of her skin, the dilation in her eyes, the raw, ripe swelling of her lips that the roughness of his kiss had caused. He'd meant to get rough with her. Meant to scare her senseless from the crazy idea of seduction that had gotten into her hard little head.

She didn't seem to understand what she was messing with. A little kissing, a sweet, slow roll in the hay simply wasn't going to slake the fire she'd struck inside him. He wasn't the tender, twenty-two-year-old lover she remembered. There was no telling if a single night of love would make things better between them. Or worse.

This time Drake seriously doubted if just one night between them would be enough.

He left her at a quiet table in the far corner of the room, then headed straight for the cash bar, returning shortly with two snifters of brandy. "A toast," he said, handing her a glass, striking the rims together, calling up a sweet, sharp sound from the clear lead crystal. "To the diamond," he told her solemnly, "and the deal we made."

They both drank, Emery taking a slow sip, Drake downing his in a single swallow. The liquid was smooth, dark, and mellow as country molasses, with an afterburn strong enough to strip paint. Drake welcomed the stinging feel of the stuff as it sizzled down his throat. Would it make him drunk? he wondered. Would it make him numb?

A man could only hope.

He whisked a chair from beneath the table, seating himself across from her. They had business left to discuss and he was ready to get down to it, cut to the chase. He was ready to resolve things with her once and for all.

"Let's get this over with, Em," he suggested casually, "now, tonight. There's too much at stake to put it off any longer. I'd like you to accept delivery on the stone immediately."

"But—that's impossible. You haven't been paid."

"I trust you," he said, "implicitly. I want you to take the diamond back to your boss and save your job. Save yourself, Emery. Swank's can send me a check later."

She stared at the thick pool of amber liquid still remaining in her glass, as if the reflection shining back at her might hold the secret answer she was looking for. But Drake knew there was no such simple answer for her to find. She would have to think with her heart this time, instead of her head.

"So, you're telling me to leave?"

"I'm telling you to save us both from what will happen if you don't. More heartache, that's all. Another messy good-bye. Is that what you want?"

She shook her head slowly. "You want this night as much as I do."

"*Woman*," he groaned. "I want it *more.*"

"Then don't make me stop. I seduced you once before, remember? Why won't you let me do it again?"

Why not? Because the consequences might be more than either of them could handle. Because he wanted to protect her from a pleasure that would ultimately end in pain. Hell, he wanted to save them *both*.

But she was equally determined to torture him with slow, sexual frustration. And doing a damn good job of it. Oxygen, Drake decided, was what he needed more of at the moment. A little less Em and a lot more air and he might just make it through the evening with his sanity.

Then again, he might not. Because he could feel himself weakening, slowly. His brain was beginning to soften to her sweet persuasion as the rest of his body grew hard. Stiff enough to break rocks with, he realized. And all they'd done was dance.

So far.

"Finish your drink, Emery," he told her. "Then come outside with me."

"Outside? What for?"

He took her by the wrist, pulled her up beside him. "You'll see."

The night was dense, full of smoke, and the sky was thick with stars. A bonfire had been set in the open field beside the auditorium, its shafts of flame shooting heavenward, licking the horizon with tall golden tendrils of heat.

"Burning leaves," Drake explained. "The first leaves of fall. Lighting them at the ball has become a kind of yearly ritual."

Emery shivered in the chill of the night air. The evening had grown darker, crisper. Colder. "It's beautiful," she murmured.

Drake's jacket was around her suddenly, warming her before the quivering had a chance to start a second time. He was behind her, his arms wrapped around her waist, his head looking over her shoulder as they watched the fire flicker and dance.

"I love the smell," she added. "It reminds me of—home."

"Chicago?"

"No. Here. Nashville."

"I see. Do you still think of Nashville as your home, Em?"

"I—I'm not sure."

"Well, you'd better make sure, pet. You need to understand this isn't your home, anymore, but it is mine. What business do I have taking you to bed again if you don't really know where you belong?"

"I *do* know where," she whispered. "At least I know where I should be tonight."

"And afterward?" he asked, determined to make her see exactly what they were up against. "I'm not into long-distance love affairs. And the legal, sign-on-the-dotted-line sort of relationship didn't work out for us too well."

"I'm not even suggesting we try that again," she insisted, shuddering. "Getting married wasn't my idea."

"Mine either," he reminded her kindly. "You know what happened between my parents, pet. And I haven't seen much since that's made me change my mind about marriage."

She gave a gentle shrug. "There won't be any

shotguns this time, if that's what you're worried about."

"What I'm worried about," he said, "is you. Wild horses wouldn't make me hurt you again, Emery. There's no Tasha to come between us anymore. I'm not a kid in need of comfort, I'm a man who wants you in the most personal way a man could want a woman. It's going to be harder to walk away this time, not easier. I want you to be aware of that."

"I am aware of it," she insisted. "And I still want to make *you* aware of me."

Drake didn't know how much longer he'd be able to hold out. He'd warned her about the consequences, heaven knew. He'd tried to warn her about himself. But she wasn't going to give up.

He was starting to think that just giving in might be the best thing for both of them. She needed to know how desirable she was, and it would be such a pleasure to show her.

The scars from that day of the ceremony were still with her, he knew. He couldn't take back the foolish words she'd overheard him say to her sister that day. But it might still be possible to help heal her now, by kissing those old wounds away.

Yes, he wanted to make it up to her. And making love would be the best way. . . .

"Go ahead," he suggested softly. "Entice me. Arouse me. Do your worst."

"What?"

"Seduce me, sweet. I can't wait to see what you have planned for us."

Emery took a deep swallow of air, caught the smell of smoke again, but even more provocative and overpowering was the scent of him. His jacket was redolent of sensual masculine spices, expensive aftershave, smooth tobacco. The satin lining of his tux was sleek against her skin. His breath was warm against her ear, hot with brandy.

"Does this mean you've changed your mind?"

"It does. I have."

"Oh!" she said, starting to break out in a fevered sweat, starting to feel sick to her stomach. She had wanted this to happen. Exactly this. But the idea of it suddenly scared her silly.

It was one thing to pretend being a mantrap, she realized, another to actually go through with it. Who was he expecting anyway? A babe in a ball-gown? Helen of Troy? He was getting her instead, Emery Brooks in vamp disguise, the woman voted most likely to sink a thousand ships.

She had no idea what to do. After all, it'd been a long time. *He'd been her only time.*

Drake wasn't the type to stay celibate for ten years. She knew there'd been others for him. He'd likely grown even better, more experienced, while she'd forgotten everything.

Actually her plan hadn't gone much beyond the dress and a few slow dances. She'd intended to show a little leg, whisper sweet nothings in his ear, that kind of stuff. She'd figured the rest would've worked itself out by now. After all, people had been doing this thing together for eons, right?

She'd been wrong. She'd been a naive, sexually inexperienced schoolgirl. And now he was expecting her to perform!

"I'm waiting, pet."

For what? she wondered. A snake dance? A slow striptease? She didn't have the slightest idea what would turn Drake Tallen on. *She didn't even know what he saw in her.*

"Tell you what," he suggested, leading her toward his car. "Let's blow this joint right now. Go back to my place. We can really get started there."

"Oh. Good idea." At least it would buy her some time. Maybe on the way back to the cavern she would think of something to do.

She didn't.

As soon as they walked inside, the dogs greeted them. But the moment of reprieve they provided Emery was short-lived. As soon as the romps and wags and greetings were over, Drake sent the canine chaperons out for an evening run.

He pulled a bottle of ice-chilled wine from the fridge by his bar and expertly uncorked it. Wine, Emery decided, was a good place to start. No decent seduction should be allowed to proceed without it. No indecent one, either.

He decanted it leisurely, handing her a tall, tulip-shaped glass full of something golden and shimmering. The drink was delicious, strangely beautiful. Tiny bits of glitter seemed to swirl through the liquid, rising and falling like thin flecks of treasure pooling at the bottom of a deep stream basin.

She held her glass up to the light, examining its contents closely. "I think there's something in mine!" she exclaimed. "It looks like—gold?"

"Correct," Drake confirmed. "It's sealed inside when the wine is bottled. King's wine, they call it. I thought this occasion deserved something special."

Wine made with pure gold? It was more than special. It was extravagant and incredibly romantic. He'd probably been saving the vintage for a very long time. He probably expected something pretty spectacular from the evening. From her.

Something she wasn't sure how to deliver. She took a long, cool swallow of the fortifying stuff. What should she do? Hop onto the coffee table and start peeling her clothes off? A little too obvious, maybe. Hardly seductive. More likely to give Drake a good laugh than make him die of desire.

"Care to take my jacket off?" he suggested.

"No, thank you. I'll just leave it on a little longer if you don't mind. I'm still a bit—"

"Shy?"

"Cold."

"No problem, then," he told her. "You have a seat on the couch. I'll set the mood. A little music, maybe? Some candlelight?"

"Of course, I mean if you'd like. Anything . . ."

"Unless you'd rather go straight to bed?"

"Straight to—" She heard her voice rising to a very unvamplike high-pitched squeak. "The music would be fine."

The sound he selected was as different as the

wine, a slow, a cappella chant, no notes, no strings, just a faint background drumbeat and the sound of voices, singing praise, in a language she couldn't understand. The candles came next. He lit about a hundred of them, tall white, in high clusters and bunches, stacking the tapers of fire around the room until the walls flickered and danced with dark purple luminescence.

He turned the lights off, took up his wine again, and watched her. Emery felt a nerve ticking slowly at the base of her throat. He was quiet as he stood there, towering over her, appearing somewhat sinister in his intentions.

The stark white shirt he wore set off the shadows in his face, throwing the planes and hollows into dramatic contrast. Satan himself would look much as he did, she realized, with green fire in his eyes, a shaded smile on his face, and lovemaking on his mind. So handsome no woman would have the power to resist.

At least, no woman would *want* to. Especially not her. She just wasn't sure how to get things going.

The seconds ticked by. The silence was excruciating. But just when Emery was about to do something really desperate, like leave, Drake saved her by speaking.

"Confess, pet," he said finally. "You're afraid."

She looked up at him, her heart crowding into her throat. He understood, thank heaven. He had all along.

"Yes," she told him, her voice heavy with relief. "Afraid of disappointing you."

"You won't," he said, "I promise. You couldn't."

"I'm not a very good seductress."

"Don't bet on that."

"Don't you see? I wanted to do something special for you tonight, be someone special."

"You always have been, Emery. Always will be. Come here, I'll prove it to you."

She hesitated, unsure, then slowly stood up from the couch.

"Come *here*, woman," he repeated, and pulled her close.

Emery got the message almost immediately. She didn't have to dance on the table, or toss her panties at him, or even play hard to get. She didn't have to do any of those absurd, very unsexy things to excite him. She only had to be herself.

Because he was aroused already.

There were parts of him pressing against her that proved it in no uncertain terms. Hard, male parts that shocked her into silence. Her heart went wildly weak.

"I want you," he said, his voice a low, sensual growl against her ear. "Just you. Just the way you are. I don't care how. There are so many ways."

He pushed her up against the wall, then, and started to show her one of them. He didn't stop to take the jacket off. He slipped his hand inside the opening and circled her breast possessively, teasing, never quite touching the dark, swollen center that had already begun to peak with arousal. Emery bit her lower lip, waiting for him to feel her there. Every fiber in her body, every shuddering nerve cell was ready for it, waiting for him to claim that aching part of her and ease the sweet pain he'd started.

A sound caught in her throat. A moan or a prayer, she wasn't sure which. His hand continued its covetous massage around the full, overflowing mound until she thought she would die of desire. The long fingers worked their way inward, closer to the taut, tender tip. They came near, so near, she could barely breathe from the anticipation. But just when she thought that he would touch her, he moved his hand to her other breast and started the erotic, expert torture all over again.

Emery cried out in sweet frustration. She arched toward him, needing more. She closed her eyes, straining, sighing, but still his fingers never found her. They just continued cupping her, splaying, stroking toward the hot turgid spot but always stopping short. She was ready to beg, she realized, ready to plead for some relief.

But just when she was almost weeping from his merciless ministrations, he reached behind her, unlatching the halter neck of her dress. He worked the zipper down next, one tight, metallic notch at a time. Gravity took control and the fabric fell away, whispering down to her waist. She was bare below his jacket, her hardened nipples painfully tight as they brushed against the raw, black silk.

He parted the satin lapels, exposing her breasts

to his view, and looked at her. His eyes grew darker, heavy, hooded with desire. A demon's eyes, Emery thought, ready to devour her with a single look.

Her breasts were so full and heavy by then, they hurt. They throbbed. If he took the peaks into his mouth at the moment, suckling them softly, assuaging her need, it would probably make her pass out. She curved toward him, *wanting* him to. *Please*, she thought silently. *Show some mercy.*

But he didn't.

"My God," he breathed, "you're beautiful."

She writhed under the sexual inspection, but her hands were caught by one of his. At the moment he wasn't allowing her to move.

"You like to hear it, pet, don't you? You like me to look at you. We don't even have to touch, do we, to make each other hot?"

"Please," she urged. "I *want* you to touch me."

But he didn't, not just yet. He was too busy watching, staring. There was something else happening that had completely caught his interest.

The involuntary twist of her body had set her dress into motion. It was starting to slide down over her hips, easing its way toward her thighs, dropping inexorably nearer the floor. Drake seemed fascinated by the garment's slow, gradual movement. He looked pleased.

But he soon grew tired of waiting. He caught a fistful of the gown, gave a single, easy yank, and it dropped in a shimmering puddle to the stone surface below. Her panty hose followed, guided by a single, sliding movement from his black magic hands. A sorcerer's hands, she thought. They'd stripped her naked in seconds and she hardly knew how.

She was still wearing the top of his tux, thank heaven, but it didn't go a long way to conceal her. Everything he seemed so interested in looking at was already showing, more or less. Which really didn't seem right because he still remained fully clothed.

"No fair," she whispered. "Now you take something off."

His voice went husky. "Sure you want me to?"

"Positive."

"All right. Just remember you asked for this."

He released her, but only for a moment, as his hands worked at unraveling the knot in his tie. It came loose, falling around his shoulders in a long, luxurious black ribbon. "There," he said, "something's off."

"Uh-uh," she told him. "You're not getting away that easy." She reached out, fumbling at his shirt studs with trembling hands, dropping the dark sapphire buttons, one by one, onto the floor. The diamond-bearing medicine bag, suspended from his neck, was the first thing she saw. "*That's* definitely going next," she said, latching on to the leather cord and slipping the small pouch over his head. "I don't even want to *think* about business or that pesky stone tonight."

She tossed the bag onto the mantel as Drake

slowly peeled his shirt off. Emery studied him boldly. After all, he'd done all the looking up to this point. But one glimpse at his chest, hard, potent, and perfect, and she felt as if her insides were coming apart.

Male nipples, she thought, could be beautiful too. She moved her mouth toward them, and kissed each of his in turn. A groan broke from inside him, making her crazy with pleasure. Her hands moved lower, across the silk of his cummerbund, stopping at the top button of his pants.

There was something very final about that button, she knew. So much raw sexual power surged below, she was almost afraid to set it free. He was rock hard, so massively male, it scared her. Once that button came open, there'd be no going back.

She moved her hand across the hardness, testing, unsure. He swore softly in her ear, but the forbidden sound of his voice only excited her further. She had power here, too, she realized. The power to bring him astonishing pleasure.

She stroked him again, her touch instinctively rhythmic. He shuddered with need, her hand seeming to set every muscle in his body in motion. Specifically, the one she'd just been exploring. It grew firmer, shocking her with its size. Just where was he going to put all that? Inside her?

Oh God, she *hoped* so.

Unhesitating, she began to work the button open.

"No way," he responded, clamping both hands over her wrists. "I can't risk letting you do that."

Before Emery fully realized what was happening, Drake had whisked the tie from his shoulders and securely wrapped it around her wrists, locking them together. He anchored the ends with a firm, fast knot. She couldn't touch him any longer. She couldn't stop him from touching her!

A tremor of fear clutched her heart. He could hurt her if he wanted. He could do anything he wanted.

The main thing Drake wanted at the moment was a chance to catch his breath. Her butterfly touches below the belt had nearly sent him over the edge. One innocent stroke from those incredible hands of hers and he was a lit stick of dynamite, ready to detonate. He couldn't let that happen, yet. Not when he was just getting started.

Not until he had her complete, undivided attention. And had driven her completely wild.

If seduction was what she wanted, he swore she was going to get it. From now on, however, *he* would be the one doing all the seducing.

The cavern flickered with firelight. It glossed the brown and copper strands of her hair with golden flashes, reflecting the depth of emotion in her eyes. Was it fear that had made the pupils dilate to dark, enormous circles, or sexual desire? He wasn't sure. But her whole body was flushed with the fire of anticipation, her legs fairly glowing, her breasts twin shimmering moons.

They shivered with movement as she tested the restraint, arms along her sides, jacket open. Her swaying was sensual, her helplessness so arousing it made his groin grip with pain. He'd tied her up for good reason. Hell, she'd been torturing him. But the sight of her satin-bound wrists was torturing him right back.

With her shoulders arched that way, her breasts swung forward, completely exposed. They were gorgeous, just made to be caressed by a man's hand. But it was her nipples that really got to him. They were dark, the pink tips flushing to a raw, taut red. They were as hard as he was, he realized, making him think of how much they both wanted this.

And how good it was going to be.

He could sense the urgency inside her as she twisted toward him, but he wasn't about to free her. He wasn't sure he could, even if he wanted to. The sight of her, fragile, vulnerable, excited him too much. He'd waited so long to have her he couldn't stop himself now.

He cupped her breasts again, this time using both of his hands. They were sweet, ripe, so erotically soft and heavy beneath his fingers, he couldn't help exploring them. He reached for the centers simultaneously, taking the nipples between his fingertips and massaging them gently, back and forth. The gasp she gave, the soft, shocked little cries, brought him amazing pleasure. He wet the peaks with his tongue, tasting his fill of each nub in turn, then drew his mouth back a few inches and blew cool currents of air across them.

He felt her knees begin to buckle beneath her, but he knelt to the floor, steadying her legs with his hands. Her thighs quivered softly as he parted them, preparing her for the further pleasures he had in store. He was nearly shaking inside himself, filled with so much rampant energy and need it took all of his skills to focus on her, instead of the white-hot ache that was flaring through his own body, setting his groin muscles on fire.

"Open up for me, Em," he told her. "Open your legs and let me touch you inside."

Emery's entire body went tense, flushing with shy embarrassment. Just the thought of Drake Tallen, kneeling on the floor before her, ministering to her softest, most private parts with his spell-weaving hands was enough to send her over the edge.

"I *can't*," she whispered.

"Do it, pet," he urged. "Don't be afraid." As if to prove just how gentle he could be, he moved his mouth to the soft copper mound that crowned the cleft between her legs and pressed his lips to the opening just below it.

The sensation was so overwhelming, Emery almost forgot to breathe. Her thighs opened instinctively, unable to resist the wild, exquisite stimulation as his tongue continued probing. She gave a tight gasp, almost overcome with the thrilling awareness of him. And just when she was least expecting it, his fingers slipped inside her, exploring deeply.

Her whole body vibrated with wanton pleasure. Her stomach muscles clutched. Her knees shook. She nearly slid to the floor.

Scooping her up in his arms, Drake carried her to the couch, seating her just at the edge. Spreading her legs wider still, he continued stroking with his long, expert fingertips, coaxing her into hypnotic submission, weaving a wild, secret spell of pure physical pleasure. She was lost in the power of his potent enchantment. Lost forever.

Still working his magic down below, he took her breast into his mouth, nipping lightly, then suckling and tugging insistently, drinking in every last drop of her. It was more than she could take. She was climaxing like crazy, shuddering and shivering with the overwhelming release of it as he took her into his arms, hugging her tight.

He took her to bed then, while every nerve ending inside her was still humming with excitement. He laid her down inside the silken tent, disappearing for a second, returning shortly with a small foil wrapper in his hand. He held the packet up, making his intentions crystal clear. "I want you, Em. But I want to protect you too. Any objections?"

She looked down at her silk-bound wrists, then smiled up at him, shooting him a provocative question with her eyes. "Not as long as I can do the honors."

"Determined?" he asked. "I was hoping you would be." He untied her wrists then, preparing himself for the excruciating ritual. In the condition he was in, the condom was going to be a tight fit. Especially since she would be the one guiding him into it.

He stretched out on the bed beside her, shuddering hard as she started to unzip his pants. Her fingers fluttered over him, hesitating, making his gut clench tight. She was enjoying herself, he realized, the moment she reached inside, freeing him from the fabric constraints. Every raw, painful, rock-hard inch.

"Emery," he groaned. "Have *mercy*."

"Why should I?" she asked him, slipping the rubber on with slow, outrageous, almost unbearable strokes. "You didn't show me any. All's fair in love and war."

Unable to respond, he bit his tongue until she'd finished, then raised himself up, kicked his pants off, and crawled toward her on all fours, menacing.

"So which one is this?" he demanded, moving over her, smiling wickedly.

"A truce?" she suggested, pretending to cower against the sheets.

She *was* a seductress, he realized. An incredibly tempting one. Tempting fate, that's what she was doing. Tempting *him*.

Luckily, he didn't have to resist any longer. Not that he could have. He had to have her now, right this minute, or the wanting was going to kill him. The fire deep inside him had leaped out of control, the feelings raging so hard, no form of mind control or meditation could stop them. She had reduced him to this, he realized. He was a hopeless case without her.

He was in danger, he knew, at serious risk of losing it all to her tonight. Mind, body, breath, *life*. But it was too late to turn back.

He kissed her fully, finally, mouth to mouth, astonished to realize it was the most emotional moment of their lovemaking. His tongue penetrated, tasting, being tasted as her lips parted, welcoming all of him in. He could feel her excitement shafting straight to his soul as she wrapped her arms around him, pulling him down toward her, urging him inside her everywhere.

He positioned himself at the crown of her thighs, seeking the opening, finding it with unerring instinct as the soft arch of her hips guided him there. He touched her with his tip, ready to impale himself in the tight, slick wetness, but wanting to make sure she was fully ready.

He entered her, but the fit was so exquisitely firm he was afraid she might tear. He fought to delay his own release, holding himself back as he cupped her bottom with his hands, taking her, with supreme male effort, one slow, searing, agonizing inch at a time. His back arched, his hips shuddered as he rotated them slowly, struggling for control.

She cried out, as aroused as he was, moving against him, impelled by an impulse of sweet, sensory surrender. She wanted more of him, all of him, and Drake promised silently she was going to get it.

Thrusting deeply, he plunged inside her, taking her to the limit of their flesh and beyond.

She began to climax again, wildly, but it wasn't simply her abandoned, bursting excitement that finally sent him over the edge. It was the way she caught hold of his shoulders, sweetly, tenderly, clinging to him as if she would never let go again.

"Drake, please," she whispered. "I need you now, inside me. Love me, Drake. Don't let go."

Longing surged through him, hard and sweet as he plunged again, rolling with her, rocking, taking her to the hilt of his passion. He was flying then, soaring with the nighthawk, only this time she was along for the ride, winging her way with him across the peaks and mountains of pleasure. They called out to each other, screaming with abandon, screeching with joy as they flew together, twirling and wheeling, talons locked as they tumbled and fell through the dark night.

Drake's physical release was the most powerful he had ever known. His body was floating, shaking, surging with a flood stronger than white water overflowing after a spring rain. But the torrent racing through him was only partly physical. More than anything, it was a climax of emotion. Their bodies had taken each other to new heights.

But it was their minds that had truly mated this time.

The mental experience was extraordinary. They had connected on a higher level, their energies touching, intertwining in the midst of an erotically altered state. It was ironic, he realized, that his own spiritual climax had occurred at the moment of their joining.

Ironic that the greatest insight of his life hadn't come from meditation, or concentration, control, or ritual. It had come from *her*. She was the reason the inner peace he'd sought had always remained elusive. She was his completion, his companion, the mate he'd been meant to connect with all his life. She had been the missing part of his spirit all along.

And he would never be whole again without her.

NINE

Emery awoke long after the candles had been extinguished, to a cavern of stunning blackness. The air was cool and dry, faintly reminiscent of smoke, the stale sweetness of wine, and the heady perfume of spent passion. The scent of it still clung to her body, to the sheets, lingering in the darkness like a soft, shadowy dream she'd had the night before. Only it wasn't a dream she remembered.

It was reality.

The wind outside had begun to howl, blowing leaves and branches against the outer door, signaling the start of a fall storm, the blustery kind that Indiana was known for in autumn. Snow would blanket the ground in a few more months, burying the leaves beneath a frosting of hard, white ice. But in spite of all that, she felt safe and secure. Not simply because of the cave's protective and luxurious comfort. Her reassurance came from the man beside her.

She heard Drake's steady breathing, calm and strong, rock solid even in sleep. He belonged here in this great Tut-like tomb, she realized, surrounded by the jeweled beauty of the place. The roots he'd buried in this cave, in this land, were deep. Living in the same area as his ancestors was the single thread of continuity that ran throughout his life.

He'd had no parents to depend on, no family to fall back on in times of trouble. His only security was here, on the acreage he'd earned for himself, in this underground fortress that served as his home. He hadn't chosen this cavern by chance. He'd picked a place to live that was permanent. So stable and solid that it would still be around hundreds of years from now.

Drake needed that kind of permanence in his life, whether he understood it or not. He was grounded in the very ground he walked on. He would never leave it, she knew.

His work at the quarry had made him rich and prosperous, financially secure, but doing well and being well weren't necessarily the same. Even a king in his golden palace required company at times. Did he ever desire companionship? she wondered. Did the fact that he'd never married mean he was just fine without that kind of long-term commitment, happier, in fact, on his own?

He'd told her as much, hadn't he? So why was she lying here thinking that a permanent relationship was the one thing missing from Drake's life? Maybe the one thing he needed the most.

Especially since she couldn't be the one to give it to him. She'd been away from Nashville for ten years. And even though the longing for the place had never completely left her, she knew it would never be her home again. At least not the way it had been, once. How could she come back here to stay and give up everything she'd worked so hard to attain? How could she return to the same small pond again and resume her role as the ugly duckling, just when she was learning how to be a swan?

But, of course, he hadn't asked her to stay.

She sat up in bed, hugging the covers around her, unable to sleep. Her body was sore in places she couldn't name, her muscles achy and weak, but still she didn't regret a second of what they'd done the night before. She hadn't ten years ago either, even though the act had finally resulted in her running away.

What would the outcome of last night's lovemaking be?

A repeat performance of the past? Should she take the diamond and run the way Drake had suggested? She wasn't sure she wanted to. After all that had happened between them, going through with the deal at this point just didn't seem right. It felt too much like making the trade he'd offered.

Too much like a betrayal.

But that was crazy, wasn't it? The business arrangement they'd made didn't have a thing to do with their lovemaking. So why did it still feel so wrong?

She rose from the bed, padding, naked, toward the bathroom. A slow soak in that warm steam pool sounded so good right about now, exactly what she needed to ease the aches in her body and, she hoped, get rid of the nagging little gremlins that were wreaking havoc with her mind.

Rough, Jack, and Rowdy awoke from their doggy dreams and followed her to the door, wistfully watching for any sign that a morning snack was about to be served.

"Sorry, guys," Emery whispered softly. "But I don't even know where the can opener is. We'll just have to wait for the big boss to get up."

She heard Drake stirring in his sleep, and glanced toward him, sighing. He was stretched out on his back, bare except for the bedcovering thrown over his waist. His body was incredibly beautiful beneath the lamplight. One arm was flung behind his head in a pose of perfect relaxation, and that black wave of hair fell across his forehead, so boyishly out of place on a man of his potent power.

It was the hair that really got to her, that small sign of residual vulnerability that made her heart crowd into her throat. She had a hard time swallowing all of a sudden, and a dull, painful ache was starting to throb behind her eyes. No matter how tough Drake looked on the outside, he wasn't as invincible as he'd like her to believe. He could still be hurt, she realized, wounded more easily than she'd ever imagined.

The thought of crawling into that bed with him

again made her understand just how much she wanted to return to the safety of his arms. Strong arms that could strike down the dragons that hounded her, soothe her concerns, and assure her that everything would work out this time. Although she had no idea how.

She turned toward the bathroom again. The faint light of dawn streamed in through the ceiling skylight as she entered the steaming tub and sank down into the warm, cleansing water. As much as she wanted to go back to that bed and lie down beside him again, she needed this time to think. The pool's soft, purling wetness ebbed and flowed around her, swirling nearly as fast as the emotions that swept through her mind.

The one that tugged at her the most was longing, a longing that her solitary life in Chicago had never been able to fulfill. She'd never realized just how strong it was until the day she'd returned home and felt the pull of the past reaching out for her again, offering something she'd missed along the way. A sense of belonging, of needing someplace.

Needing someone.

Was it possible that Drake needed her as well? Or did he intend to stick to their deal unconditionally? Why had one night with him forced her to take a second look at the choices she'd made?

Because it had been like no night she had ever known. The connection between them had been more than merely physical. The experience had been pure magic. It wasn't just their bodies that had touched. Their minds had joined as well, soaring off together to some dark, starlit place. Drake Tallen hadn't simply made love to her. He'd penetrated her soul.

Running away from him this time would be different, harder than before, and far more painful. This time she would have to leave a piece of herself behind. The idea of it ripped at her, tore at her heart.

But it seemed there were no other options.

Drake yawned heavily, rolling out of bed and stretching, pantherlike, as soon as he hit the floor. The aching in his muscles as he pulled and tested them was a welcome reminder of the woman who'd tested his endurance. Luckily for both of them his body had finally given in, but the experience of holding back for such a prolonged period of time was definitely character building.

A man could always use a little more character.

He glanced to her side of the bed, wondering how she'd feel about picking up where they left off, but the spot where she'd lain beside him was empty.

"Emery?"

He stopped by his chest of drawers for a pair of shorts, pulling them on with a slight grimace, then strolled into the great room. Her dress still lay in a glittering pile on his stone floor where it had dropped the night before. He picked up the small piece of fabric and held it to his face, inhaling her scent. The memory made him smile. It made him hard.

He'd known one night with her would never be enough. So much for the cleansing ritual they'd hoped for the evening to be. She'd offered him purification, closure. But it hadn't worked.

This thing he had for her was chronic. It was incurable.

It was love.

Love, dammit! He didn't even believe in the lasting effects of it. He'd imagined he was in love with Tasha once, too, and he'd been wrong about that. His folks must've thought they loved each other at one time, but that hadn't stopped them from busting up later, and leaving him behind.

Which was why he'd sworn it wasn't going to happen to him.

But he didn't miss the bitter irony of the fact that he'd fallen in love with Emery Brooks. He guessed he deserved to be devastated emotionally by the woman he'd hurt before. But he wasn't about to let her see just how perfect her payback was, even though he knew it hadn't been intentional.

She'd already shredded his ego once before, stomped it all to hell with the hard soles of her size-seven shoes. He wasn't going to lay it out in front of her this time just so she could walk all over it again.

On her way back to Chicago.

No thank you, pet.

"Emery?" Where was she, the dangerous little heartbreaker? Somewhere in his home, no doubt, running loose. After all, she couldn't leave without her clothes. She didn't even have a car.

The sight of the dogs lined up outside the bathroom door, patiently waiting with their heads between their paws, finally clued him in. He heard the sound of splashing water. Ah, she was bathing. Naked in his small, steaming pool. Why was the idea of that so incredibly appealing? His sexual hunger for her should've been quenched after last night.

It wasn't. How many other ways were there to have her that he'd overlooked? Dozens and dozens. Did he still want her? Very, very badly.

It was the emotional hunger that had him worried the most, though. How was he going to survive another ten years without her? Talk about spiritual endurance tests. But he would have to prepare himself to take it. He had no other choice.

There was no way he was going to beg her to stay this time.

But when he pushed open the door and caught sight of her soaking languidly in his pool, he came pretty close to doing just that. Begging.

"Em," he said, his voice growing hoarse. "There you are."

Looking startled by his sudden appearance, she sank the top half of her body back under the water, still a bit nervous with him. Her breasts bobbed to the surface, making simple speech incredibly difficult for him. "Care for some breakfast?" he managed.

Food was actually the last thing on his mind at

the moment, but he wouldn't want that beautiful body of hers to waste away to nothing. He wanted to help her keep her strength up. There was no telling when she might need it again.

"Oh, maybe just a cup of coffee?" she suggested, not meeting his eyes.

Was it shyness that had made her look away like that, he wondered, or something else? Something far worse. Was she ready to leave already? To end it here and now?

Oh hell, was this the kind of thing that happened when you really fell hard for a woman? Did you start second-guessing yourself at every turn, reading hidden meaning and nuance into each innocent movement she made? He exhaled heavily. *Control*, he thought. *Concentration.*

"One cup of coffee coming up," he promised her. "But you'll be sorry you missed my champagne-and-apple omelet."

Just not as sorry as he was. He took the shimmering scrap of a dress he still held in his hand and hung it on the hook inside the bathroom door. "There's a spare robe in the closet if you need it," he added, heading for the kitchen.

She would definitely need it. Because if she showed up wearing nothing but that outfit again, he wasn't sure he'd have the strength to drive her back to Tasha's house. And tell her good-bye for good.

Self-pity. He was wallowing in it already. But he wasn't going to make this harder on both of them than it had to be. He'd known what he was getting himself into. He'd gotten what he'd asked for.

And she had accomplished what she came here for.

Ten minutes later Emery walked into the room, talking fast, still not looking him square in the eye. "I called Tasha to let her know where I was. She's coming to pick me up in a few minutes, and her car *does* have four-wheel drive, so you don't have to worry about taking me home. I'd call a cab, but I might look a little weird wearing *this*," she said, indicating the oversized terrycloth robe she'd thrown on over her dress. "And I really wouldn't feel safe in a taxi anyway," she added. "Not since I'll be carrying the diamond."

He knew she was trying to let him down easy, work her way into it, get out graciously this time. But there was no polite way to tear a man's heart in two. And he really didn't want her pity. She was only prolonging the inevitable. He had to stop her, put an end to it.

He handed her a cup of coffee. "Just tell me one thing, Em. What are you going to do now? Go back to Chicago?"

But he didn't have to wait for her answer. He already knew. He'd known all along.

She nodded, fighting back the tears. "Yes."

He forced himself to smile. "So that's it, then? Don't call us, we'll call you? The check's in the mail?"

"We both knew it would end up this way," she

whispered, the tears beginning to flow. "You can't go. I can't stay."

"No," he agreed. "Naturally not. But since you *are* going, pet, I suggest you do it soon, while I'm still thinking straight." He crossed the great room, reaching the mantel, taking the pouch from the spot where they'd left it. He dumped the diamond out and carried it back to her, dropping it onto her open palm. "Don't take any chances," he told her. "Go now. There's no telling what could happen with the curse. The stone might be affected somehow, since I'm feeling a little angry."

A *little* angry? He was ready to knock the walls down with his fists. But since they were transferring ownership of the stone, he was pretty sure that Emery would be safe, no matter what kind of repercussions his wrath might cause.

"At me?" she asked him, swallowing back a sob.

"At myself," he admitted.

She stepped forward to touch his face, her hand trembling. "Drake—I'm sorry."

He caught her by the fingertips and pulled them to his lips, kissing her there, one last time. "Don't be," he told her. She had nothing to be sorry for.

Nothing at all.

A car pulled up outside, its engine humming over the sound of the wild, raging windstorm. "Just go," he added, turning his back on her so she wouldn't see the effort that the words had cost him. "Go on, pet. Get out of here. Good-bye."

❖───────❖

"Jeez, Emery, are you okay?"

Tasha asked the question on their way back to the house, while Emery, still wearing the oversized bathrobe and the crushed ballgown beneath it, sat in the front seat beside her, sobbing her eyes out.

"No," she admitted between bursts of uncontrollable weeping. "Actually, I'm not."

She was tired, heartsick, and so confused she couldn't think straight. The diamond was still clutched in her hot little hand. She was gripping it so hard, the corners were starting to cut into her skin. But what difference did a little pain make? She had what she'd come here for. She should feel happy. Proud.

She felt like throwing up.

She felt like taking the horrid, cursed rock and throwing it straight into Mia Swank's selfish, smirking face.

But she couldn't. Not if she wanted to keep her job and her self-esteem along with it. Oh, yes, it would give her a great deal of satisfaction to drive back to the big city and walk into Swank's, showing off the prize she'd secured for the store. She would return triumphant, successful.

And sick to her stomach.

"What happened?" Tasha prompted, her voice full of concern.

"Nothing." Emery sniffed. "Everything. Oh, I

don't know! I think I'm going crazy. Maybe the diamond's having some sort of effect on me."

But she knew what was affecting her. It was glittering and green, and strikingly, sinfully beautiful. Only, it wasn't the diamond. It was the look of passion in Drake's eyes when he'd made love to her. The look of pain as he tried to shut her out when she'd left.

She would never forget either one as long as she lived. "It's Drake," she confessed. "Oh, Tasha, I've done a terrible thing."

Her sister's glance grew skeptical. "It can't be that bad, whatever it is," she said, frowning. "You're not capable of doing anything *too* awful."

"I didn't realize what I was capable of until I came back here," she admitted. "God, I've been such a fool." She unfisted her hand, holding the stone up to the light so Tasha could get a good look at it. "I sold myself," she said. "For this."

Tasha's eyes widened in surprise. "You did what?"

"I *sold* myself," she repeated. "For a rock. For nothing."

She should never have taken the gem from him at all, she decided. It was his talisman, his protective charm. They were connected, Drake and this diamond. Selling it to Swank's made her feel as though she were selling a piece of him.

She was selling out.

But they'd had an agreement, hadn't they? He didn't need the diamond to survive. He was strong without it, always had been. There was really no reason she should feel so bad. It was only business. *Her* business. Her career, her life.

"You—sold yourself?" Tasha repeated. "You didn't. I don't believe it."

Emery nodded solemnly, shaking her head with self-disgust. "I did, I swear it."

"Emery, I still don't understand. Slow down and take a deep breath. Are you saying you spent the night with Drake Tallen to get that diamond?"

"No, no. I mean, yes, I slept with him. But not for the diamond. He'd already agreed to sell it to me. This morning was when I sold out, when I took it with me."

"But he's being paid for it, isn't he?"

"Yes! But it's not the money. Don't you see? It's *me*. I left him for this diamond. For everything it represents. I hurt him to save my job."

"I don't see how you had any choice. Besides, how do you know he's hurt?"

Emery glanced out the car window, studying the darkening, storm-tossed sky above. "I can't explain it entirely. I can just feel it. We're—connected somehow. We connected last night."

"Obviously," Tasha responded, smiling.

"Tasha, it was *amazing*."

"Emery!"

"Well, it was. *He's* amazing. He showed me the most incredible thing."

"Okay, that's it. If you start naming *any* of Drake

Tallen's anatomical parts, I'm going to pull this car over and let you walk home!"

"Too late," Emery murmured, half smiling. "We're already at the house. And that wasn't what I was going to say anyway."

What she'd meant was that Drake had touched her in a way no other man ever would. He had shown her *herself*. A person she was just beginning to get acquainted with.

Someone she didn't much like at the moment.

But maybe she was being too hard on herself. Maybe she just needed to get her life back on track again, get back on the road to Chicago as soon as possible. Being away for all this time was likely her only problem. She'd never questioned the course of her career before leaving, never doubted the direction she was headed in. All she had to do now was point herself back toward her own personal destiny. Whatever that was.

She followed Tasha inside the house. "Thanks for listening," she told her.

"Feel any better?"

"A little. Talking helped. But I think I know something else that will work. Mind if I use your phone?"

"To call him?"

"No," Emery said firmly, shaking her head. "To call Mia and give her the news. I can hardly wait to hear what she has to say."

"Easy, boy."

Drake reined the stallion in from the wild gallop they'd just made across the endless stretch of valley. He and Stealth had been racing together for what seemed like hours now, flying with the wind, free and reckless and entirely alone. They were both sheened with sweat from the effort, both physically spent, and it was past time he gave his loyal horse a much-needed break.

Past time he stopped running himself.

Sooner or later he would have to stand and face the truth. He was alone again. She was gone, this time for good.

Taking the horse through its cooling paces, a canter first, then a slow, easy trot, Drake decided that isolation had its advantages. Peace. Quiet. Plenty of time to contemplate the meaning of the universe. Time to find something left of the meaning of his own life.

Without her.

He'd had challenges in his day before. A childhood spent as an outsider, parents he hadn't been able to depend on. Those were the biggest obstacles he'd faced and fought and, eventually, overcome.

But the strength and persistence that had taken him to the top were nothing compared with the inner will and determination he needed now.

The wisest man he'd ever known, his grandfather, had taught him that the biggest challenges in life are the ones we set for ourselves. Only now, at what was possibly the lowest point in his life, could he completely understand the meaning of the old man's words. He'd started on a vision quest many years ago to find peace within himself.

He'd found *her*, instead.

He'd found love.

And in the process of discovering it, he'd sacrificed part of himself. A part he had to learn to live without. Going on without Emery would likely be the greatest challenge of his life, mainly because the outcome of it seemed inevitable.

It seemed hopeless.

Dismounting from the stallion, Drake caught hold of the reins and led the animal to the murky, swiftly flowing stream of Indian Creek. The recent storm had raised the level of it several inches, stirring up sediment from the rocky bottom, increasing the velocity as well. The sky spirits had been restless, angry, and the earth was reacting to them with a force of her own. The cycle was as endless as the loneliness of the life that stretched before him.

The simple certainty of his own future should, at the very least, bring him some sense of relief. But it didn't. Was there some small trace of hope left he'd overlooked?

His mind screened back over the past week, stopping, not surprisingly, on the night of their lovemaking. It was that first moment of penetration he thought of now. Why? What had he forgotten?

He'd been too preoccupied to think about it then, too caught up in the ecstasy of their joining, but he called up the memory again now and tried to remember what had surprised him so. Yes, there had been something. . . .

It was the way their bodies had fit. The sweet, shocking tightness that had brought him so much pleasure. She'd been small, so small, she'd surprised a sense of wonder from him. Virginal, that's how she'd felt. The innocence of it had excited him beyond belief, but it had also raised a tantalizing question in his mind.

Was it possible there had been no other men for her in the past ten years? Had he been the only one? If it were true, the step she'd taken by sleeping with him again was even greater than he'd first imagined. That night must have meant as much to her as he'd wanted it to.

Or was he merely grasping at straws, hoping that she would, by some miracle, change her mind about leaving? Either way, it was out of his hands. Whatever course Emery took now, it was a choice that was entirely hers to make.

Thirty minutes later he arrived back at the cavern, just in time to hear his phone ringing. The sound of it made the muscles in his gut clench tight, another side effect he'd have to get used to. The kind of thing a man had to endure after a woman walked away with his heart. He cursed softly, promising himself perfect control over his pulse the next time the noise sounded. He picked up the receiver, swearing he didn't give a damn who was on the other end.

"Drake?"

TEN

The voice Drake heard at the other end of the line was definitely female but not the one he'd been hoping for.

"Drake? Are you there? It's Tasha."

The disappointment was as fierce as a swift, sudden kick to the solar plexus. He exhaled slowly. "Tasha. What can I do for you?"

"I was hoping you could stop by the shop for a few minutes," she explained. "I'm here right now. It won't take long, but we have to talk."

About what? Drake wondered. Undoubtedly, it had something to do with her sister, but he wasn't sure he wanted to hear what Tasha had to say. If the news had been good, Emery would definitely have called herself.

"Worried about me, Tasha?" he asked, not unkindly. "Don't be. Can't we just handle it over the phone?"

She hesitated. "Actually, no. I need to see you. The sooner the better."

Drake wanted to remind her of all the trouble she'd gotten him into the last time they talked, but he didn't have the heart. Her intentions had been good, which was more than he'd learned to expect from her before.

"What is it?" he asked her. "Some kind of message?"

"Well—sort of. Emery left something behind for you on her way back to Chicago. I promised I'd give it to you in person."

On her way back to Chicago. The words lanced through him as sharply as a long steel blade slashing through the line. So that was it, then. The break was final. She'd made her decision and followed through with it. There was no hope left.

There was only a morbid, sick kind of curiosity inside him that still wanted to know what she'd written him.

"Don't go anywhere," he told her. "I'll be right over."

Tasha smiled at him sweetly as he crossed the threshold of her shop. Almost too sweetly, Drake decided suspiciously. She had the sympathetic expression of a hospital nurse advancing toward him with a long, businesslike needle. *Don't worry*, her eyes told him gently. *This won't hurt a bit.*

He didn't want to be curt with her, but he

couldn't seem to help himself. He *had* to see it now, immediately. "Where's the note?"

Her eyebrows drew together in a puzzled frown. "The note? I don't think I know about any note. Was there supposed to be one?"

She didn't know about it? What the devil did she mean? She'd just *called* him about it, hadn't she? "The letter," he amended, as patiently as was humanly possible. "The message from Emery."

"Oh!" Her wide blue eyes lit up in sudden comprehension. "The *message*. Did you think it was a letter? It's not. I hope you won't be disappointed. In fact, it's not really a message, either. I told her she should enclose some kind of explanation for you, but she said you'd understand."

Drake choked back a groan of frustration. Tasha was an attractive woman, he had to give her that, but her complete lack of logic was quietly driving him crazy. If there was no note from Em, then what was it? He wasn't sure whether to be relieved or disappointed as he watched Tasha walking toward the cash register.

Money? That was it, most likely. Emery had managed to get the check here early, somehow. *She was paying him off quickly so she wouldn't prolong the pain.*

How efficient, he thought. What a good businesswoman she was. What a thoughtful, thorough little heartbreaker.

At least the cut would be clean this time. Quick. The bells on the machine chimed melodically as

Tasha inserted her key and opened the drawer. Drake recognized the first six notes of the "Wedding March." Nice touch, he thought. The final turn of the knife.

He felt the bile rising in his throat and turned his back so Tasha wouldn't see the involuntary tightening of his jaw.

"This is the safest place I could think of to keep it," she explained. "Frankly, I didn't even want the responsibility but—Drake? Are you okay?"

He drew in a deep breath, regaining control. Just long enough, he estimated, to get himself out of there without becoming physically sick. He whipped around again to face her. "I'm fine, Tasha. Just fine. Now, if you'll just hand me the—"

He stopped in mid-sentence, completely confused at what she was holding in the palm of her hand. It was the diamond. The stone that should've been long gone to Chicago by now. How the hell had it ended up here?

"You take it," Tasha told him. "It makes me nervous just having it around."

Drake reached out wordlessly, relieving her of the unwanted responsibility, then stared down at the gem in his hand, thunderstruck. "*This* is what she left for me? What about the deal with Swank's? What about her job?"

"What job?" Tasha asked him, smiling. "She quit. Right after Mia fired her over the phone."

"She was fired?" he asked, glancing momentarily

at Tasha, then back down at the stone. "Because of this," he said with sudden certainty. "Am I right?"

When he looked up again, Tasha nodded. "Because she refused to bring the diamond back with her."

Drake shook his head in disbelief. "But she knew that was exactly what would happen if she didn't follow through on our deal. Tasha, why didn't she follow through?"

"You're asking me? She said you'd understand. All I know is, Emery felt the stone should stay with you. She said she just didn't feel right about going ahead with it, something about a conflict of interest. But Mia hit the roof. Apparently, she still wants it if you'd still like to sell."

Drake narrowed his eyes dangerously. "I wouldn't sell swampland to Mia Swank. Tasha, why did Emery go back to Chicago if she knew she'd already been fired?"

"Oh, that's an easy one. She only went to collect her things. She's moving into the house with me until she decides what to do next."

Drake shoved the diamond carelessly into the side pocket of his pants. He could barely believe what he was hearing.

Why? She'd told Tasha that he would understand and he did, in part. Giving up her job had to have been a great sacrifice. So much of her self-worth came from it, he knew she hadn't simply ditched it without a good reason. But what was that reason? Had she been afraid of hurting him, afraid he might misinterpret her motives for the night they'd spent together? Or did it mean something more?

Maybe it was her way of telling him she didn't intend to run away again. Ever.

He thought of the stone in his pocket and how it had brought him hope. First, on the occasion when he'd found it, and now, when it had found him again. Both times had brought him incredible luck. Whether it had been sent to him or he had been sent to find it made little difference. There was no doubt in his mind now that the Devil's Diamond had fulfilled its destiny.

And he finally understood what he had to do to fulfill his.

It was a daunting discovery, Emery decided, to find out that all of your possessions fit easily inside the five-by-eight storage space of a rented minivan. It was a humbling experience, far worse than being fired. Actually, making that fateful phone call to Mia and immediately getting canned for it had felt pretty good.

Gross insubordination, that's what Ms. Swank had called it, but Emery knew she'd done the right thing. Oddly enough, she'd felt relieved afterward, as if a weight had been lifted from her shoulders. She'd felt free.

Now she simply felt scared.

For the first time in a very long time she was

facing the unknown. It was exciting, euphoric, and terrifying all at once. But she was heading *home*.

Fear had kept her from returning to Nashville for all these years—not a fear of the town, but of what she would revert to if she ever went back. She never wanted to be that insecure, unsure-of-herself teenage girl again, the little sister who'd always taken a backseat to Tasha. But she'd finally learned that reliving the past wasn't even a possibility. She wasn't the same girl she had been ten years ago. Her visit to Nashville had taught her that.

He had taught her that.

She was a vibrant, self-assured woman, beautiful in many ways. He had seen it in her all along, had helped her see it in herself.

And she loved him for it.

She had *always* loved him, but never like this. Her attraction for Drake, her adolescent adoration, had grown into something deeper, more fulfilling. She was strong enough to bring more of herself to a relationship with him.

If there even was a relationship left. The risk she'd taken was tremendous, she realized. He might not even want her back. Maybe the one night had been enough for him. But an entire lifetime still wouldn't be enough for her.

Even if it was over for them, she would still never regret what she'd done. She'd put the past behind her, and one way or another, she was moving ahead. Looking forward this time, instead of back.

Pulling the van in front of the bridal shop, where

she knew Tasha was expecting her, she put the vehicle in park and cut the engine. The long trip was finally over, but the real adventure was just beginning.

A "Closed" sign hung in the window and the shop was deserted, even though it was early afternoon. Strange, especially since her sister had known what hour she'd be arriving, and it wasn't at all like Tasha to neglect her business. Stepping outside, she walked to the front of the store and peered inside. At least the lights were on. She tried the door, but it was locked tight.

She turned to leave, vaguely wondering if it was inventory time and whether or not she should try the back delivery entrance as well. But the sound of the front door opening behind her put those questions to rest. She spun around, expecting Tasha's smiling face. She saw Drake Tallen instead.

"Drake! I—I came here to see—where's Tasha?"

She was babbling, she knew, but he'd caught her by surprise. What was he doing here, anyway? Not that it mattered, she couldn't have been happier to see him. She had the strongest urge to run forward and fling herself into his arms. She quelled it with an effort, reminding herself she had no right.

"Tasha's on an errand," he explained calmly. "I offered to wait here for you instead."

"Oh!" So then he'd known she was on her way back. He'd understood she was jobless, homeless, with everything of importance to her crammed clumsily into the back of a rattling rent-a-van.

Looking up at him now, into that proud, perfect face of his, she realized that none of that mattered. *He* was the only thing of importance left in her life.

She could only pray he *was* still in her life.

He caught her by the wrist, propelling her inside the store, shutting the door behind them. "I heard what you did," he said suddenly, gently, taking both of her hands in his larger ones and squeezing them tight. "Tasha told me everything."

A hard, aching lump was starting to form at the base of Emery's throat as she looked up at him. She caught a quick glimpse of sweet, searing, male need in his eyes. Why was he staring at her as if he wanted to sweep her into the safety of his arms and never let go? Was it possible that his heartstrings were stretched as tautly as hers, hurting so badly they were almost at the breaking point?

"Everything, huh?" she murmured. He didn't know the half of it. He didn't know how she'd lain awake these last few nights, restless, sleepless, thinking only of him. Or how the sound of his voice could send her heart soaring with a few simple words. *He didn't know how much she loved him.*

He tucked a hand under her chin, tilting her head up until she had nowhere else to look but into his bright, burning gaze. "Enough to make me crazy with curiosity, Em. Just enough to give me hope. But I need to hear the rest from you."

Emery's heart leaped into her throat, filling it up so completely, there wasn't room left to speak. He wasn't the only one reaching out to grasp that last shred of hope. But she wasn't sure at this point how to catch on to it.

What could she tell Drake now that she hadn't already shown by action and deed? What did she have left to give him except her word of honor that she loved him, and a solemn promise that she always would? But that was exactly the kind of vow she'd never taken before. The kind he'd never wanted to take with her. Was he ready now to give them both another chance?

He took her by the shoulders, giving them an urgent little shake, as if he could barely wait to hear what she had to say. "Emery," he coaxed. "What made you change your mind?"

She found her voice then, thank goodness, found the strength to answer him. The strength that had been inside her all along. "It didn't feel right," she explained slowly, her voice trembling with the emotions that were overflowing inside her. "Something told me not to go through with it, and I just— *couldn't*. I didn't want you to think that our—that what happened between us had anything to do with the deal or my job. It definitely did not. It was special. Very—personal."

His fingertips tightened against her skin at the sound of her words, as if they were exactly what he'd needed to hear. As if he were fighting for control of his own emotions as well. "You did it for me, pet?"

She let out a sigh, her insides still tremulous, her voice soft and shaky. "Partly. I did it for myself as well. It was time for me to stand up to Mia's demands, to make a change. I guess I did it for *us*."

Drake pulled her into his arms and hugged her, holding her so tight, she could barely catch her breath.

"I'm proud of you," he said, kissing her forehead, lifting his lips to her hair with a tenderness she'd never known.

She hugged him back, clutching his broad, muscled body as several tears squeezed out of her eyes. "For getting myself fired?" she murmured into his chest, managing a little laugh. "Yeah, I did that pretty well, don't you think?"

He held her for several more moments, stroking her hair, bringing them both the kind of secure, physical assurance and comfort they craved. When his heart slowed to a steady hammer, he drew back, studying her face. "I'm sorry you lost your job, but not that sorry. I never wanted you to leave, Em. I never realized how much I would miss you until you did."

She closed her eyes. The sounds of his words were so sweet, she wanted to savor them, drink them in slowly. "You—missed me?"

He laughed, but his voice was full, fierce. "Like nobody's business."

Emery's eyes blinked open again and she looked up at him in wonder. There were so many things written across his handsome face, she could hardly take them all in at once. The pain of the past, the promise of the future. He had always been a man who lived by his own rules, who followed through with the strength and certainty of his own convictions. A man who had the guts to be himself.

"I love you," she told him, letting the tears flow freely.

He grinned. "Pet, don't make it look so painful. At least one of us is happy about it."

She laughed, wiping the moisture from her face. "You?"

"Definitely me. Because it stacks the odds in my favor this time. And if a man has to face rejection, he'd just as soon minimize the risk."

Emery sniffed back the tears, slightly confused. "What risk?"

"The possibility you'll still say no to the question I'm about to ask."

Her breath caught. What was that question? The one she'd wanted to hear from Drake Tallen her entire life but never had?

"No guts, no glory," she whispered with a trembling, terrified smile.

"Here goes, then," he said, getting down on one knee before her, his black hair gleaming like midnight as it caught the light of the crystal chandelier. He gazed up at her, but all trace of humor had fled from his eyes. His expression was so sincere, so heartfelt and serious, it almost hurt to look at him.

But she did look at him. She wouldn't have torn her gaze away for anything, even if she could have.

"Emery, will you marry me?"

She was crying again. "Yes," she whispered simply, "I will."

She tried to pull him up, wanting to hold him again, to be held, but he wasn't moving. "Not yet," he told her as a flash of a smile crossed his face. "I never had a chance to do this before, and I intend to do it right."

She smiled. "You already have. I thought it was *perfect.*"

"Speaking of perfect . . ." From somewhere inside the dark, soft flannel shirt he wore, he pulled a small black pouch. Not the medicine bag he'd carried the diamond in, but something smaller, fancier, sewn from velvet, embroidered with gold. He tipped it upside down, dropping a bright, glittering piece of jewelry onto the palm of his hand.

A ring.

Emery let out a soft sigh as he kissed each one of her fingertips in turn, finally slipping the delicate band onto the third finger of her left hand. It wasn't just any ring, she realized. It was an engagement ring, and the stone that sparkled from the center of it was so radiant, it nearly took her breath away.

"I love you, pet," he told her, still kneeling on the floor before her, holding her hand to his face, stroking the soft, sensitive skin across his lips. "I always will."

He stood up, kissing her again, this time pressing the warmth of his mouth to hers as she let out a moan at the pleasure of it. He deepened the touch, making their contact more tender, so intimate that it started a slow burn deep inside her that was hot and familiar.

But just when things were starting to get really good, he pulled back. "You really want to this time?"

She nodded vehemently, then tilted her head back so he could kiss her again.

"Not *that*," he said with an easy laugh, chucking her playfully under the chin. "I mean marriage. You do intend to go through with it, don't you?"

"I do." She clasped her hands in front of her face, prayerlike.

"You'd better."

"I swear it," she breathed.

"And your career?" he asked, still not perfectly satisfied. "Have you made any plans for that?"

"Nothing definite," she explained. "But there are several nice jewelry stores in town. I'm sure their styles are more relaxed than Swank's, less ritzy, but it might be fun to work in an environment like that for a while."

"Only if you want to," he told her.

"Well, I do intend to stay involved with some aspect of gemology." She grinned up at him. "Who knows, maybe I'll take up diamond hunting for my new career."

"Still tempted to check out the creek again?" he teased. "That's what I get for marrying a rock hound. One diamond just isn't enough."

"This one is," she said as her new ring caught her eye again. It felt good on her hand, slightly strange and heavy, but comforting, too, and best of all, permanent. The stone in the middle of the feminine filigree mounting was so blinding, she simply had to take a closer look. She lifted it toward her face, staring in awe and wondrous surprise. It wasn't just gorgeous.

It was green.

"Oh!" she exclaimed. "You had it cut!"

He nodded. "It was the least I could do if we're going to be lifetime partners. As the Devil's Diamond, it did give me a certain, unfair—advantage. It's yours now, pet. No more curses. This way the power between us is in perfect balance."

The diamond flashed brilliantly, catching the overhead light in a spectacular display. Drake glanced down at it, frowning slightly. "Do you like the ring, Em?" he asked. "Because if it makes you the least bit uncomfortable . . ."

Her jaw dropped and she smiled, shaking her head. "Are you kidding? It's the most beautiful one I've ever seen, and I've seen a lot. But the significance of it is even more important. Did you know the marriage ring is worn on the third finger because the ancients believed a 'vein of love' ran from there straight to the heart?"

His dark eyebrows arched at her in amusement. "So I'm not the only one in our family who believes in folklore?"

"Folklore?" she asked, lifting herself on tiptoe to whisper something secret in his ear. "You made me believe in magic."

He cradled her against him, and the secure, sensual warmth of his body heat reminded Emery of something else she wanted to say. "Drake?"

"Hmmm?" he responded, kissing her lightly along the underside of her chin, teasing her with his lips, working them gradually toward the tender, ticklish nape of her neck.

"Drake, I was just wondering . . . ?"

"Yes?"

"What made you change your mind about getting married?"

"Your captivating charms, my pet," he murmured, barely lifting his mouth from the base of her throat.

"Drake, I'm serious!"

He drew back and looked at her. "So am I, sweet. But if you need more reassurance about just how *much* I want to marry you, I'll try to explain."

"Please," she prompted.

"You know I've been pretty disillusioned about the wedding thing," he told her. "First from my folks, then from the time I thought I wanted to marry Tasha, then when *you* dumped me at the last minute, I decided I'd had enough of the whole idea of I do."

Emery swallowed hard. "I know. So what makes you sure it's going to work out between us?"

"There is no sure thing," he said honestly. "But I'd say the odds are in our favor this time. Not many couples have known each other as long as we have, pet. And then there's the fact that we started out as friends. I've always *liked* you, Em. Even before I fell in love with you."

She smiled. "I think I *lusted* for you first, *then* fell in love."

He chucked her lightly under the chin. "And all along I thought you were such an innocent little thing. Until that night . . ."

"It *was* a long time ago," she said, slightly defensive.

"Very long," he agreed. "But, Emery, I think I know something you haven't shared with me yet. A secret you've been keeping. You've been innocent *since* that night, haven't you?"

"I—" She looked away from him swiftly, suddenly shy. How had he figured *that* out? she wondered. "Did it show that much?" she murmured, embarrassed.

What must he think of her? Some sophisticated big-city girl she'd become. Too bad it wasn't chic to stay celibate for so long. But sex wasn't the kind of thing a girl-next-door like her took lightly. And Drake was the only man she'd ever wanted to be with in that way.

"I didn't realize you'd be able to tell," she added softly, still not looking at him. "How mortifying."

"How provocative, my pet. What a sexy secret you've kept hidden away. Discovering that was even sweeter than finding the diamond."

"You like that about me?" she asked, glancing up at him.

"I love that about you, Em. A man couldn't ask

for more loyalty than the kind you've given me. What better way for me to finally realize that a marriage between us will work? When I eventually figured out that I was the only lover you'd ever had, I finally understood you were the only woman I wanted. Correction," he continued. "You *are* the only woman. And I promise I'm going to do everything in my power to be loyal right back. In fact, I *swear* I'm going to be monogamous to you, pet. As often as possible."

"Starting *now?*" she suggested softly.

He shot her a slow understanding grin. "As much as I would like to oblige you, my sweet, we still have some wedding plans to discuss."

Her eyes widened in surprise. "So soon? Can't they wait just for a little while?"

"Getting cold feet already?"

She folded her arms across her chest, tilting her chin up in stubborn, defiant determination. "Not a chance! I'm ready to tie the knot anytime you say. I'm ready *now*."

Drake's smile grew wider. "I was hoping you'd feel that way. Because now is exactly the moment I had in mind. Or, an hour from now to be more precise."

Emery blinked in confusion. "Excuse me?"

"No excuses this time," he warned her. "Remember that errand I told you Tasha was on? Well, she should be about finished by now."

"Finished? With what?"

"With the preparations for our wedding. She

helped me plan it. I hope you don't feel rushed, pet, but I think I've waited for this day long enough. And I don't intend to give you too much time to change your mind."

"You're serious!"

He nodded. "Perfectly. All you have to do is slip on that dress she's laid out for you in the back room and meet me at the altar in an hour."

Her heart was racing again suddenly. He wanted to marry her now, today. This was her wedding day! How was she ever going to get ready for it? "Which altar?" she asked breathlessly. "Where?"

"Your instructions are next to the gown," he said calmly, kissing her on the cheek before he started to walk out the door again. "A car will pick you up in forty-five minutes." He stopped briefly, turning back toward her with a slow, hesitant smile. "And Emery . . ."

"Yes?"

"If you want a happy ending this time, you're going to have to finish the entire ceremony to see how ours turns out."

EPILOGUE

When Drake watched the long black limousine pull up to the forest clearing, his first reaction was one of incredible, overwhelming relief. If his luck held out, it was really going to happen this time. Emery Brooks would finally be his to cherish, honor, and love. Yes, *love*. Emotionally, physically, in every way he could imagine. He could definitely promise her plenty of that.

But as soon as the door opened and Emery stepped out, all rational thought was swept away by the sight of her. She was ethereal, elegant in a full foaming gown of white, its train swirling around her ankles in a floating whirlpool of wind and autumn leaves. Her hair flowed freely around her face, wild and natural, as golden-flecked and copper-rich as the tree-studded hills that surrounded them.

She was beautiful, his fall bride. He only hoped

she'd stick around long enough this time to become his wife.

He stepped forward, offering his arm, and they walked together through the wooded clearing to the altar he'd made from rough-hewn logs. It was covered now with branches and berries, strewn with the hundreds of wildflowers that her two attendants, Tasha and Electra, had collected. They would be the only witnesses. Her sister, his friend, and the soft-spoken justice of the peace he'd asked to perform the private, legal ceremony.

Their spiritual joining, Drake knew, had already taken place.

The wind whispering through the treetops, the birds singing above were the only notes of music that marked the recital of their wedding vows. Drake flew through his without a hitch, then held his breath until she spoke the two most amazing words.

"I do."

Peace flowed through him at the sound as he reached the culmination of his quest. Peace, followed shortly by the sweet, escalating passion of their kiss. He would take her home tonight, back home with him where she belonged, and finally, fully, take her again. She was his from now on, his Em, his woman, his wife.

Emery kissed him back freely, hoping that if this wedding was a dream, it was one she would never wake from. Tasha had planned it so perfectly, with nothing to remind them of that awful, almost-ceremony of the past. Their vows today had been sweet and short, their kiss long, languid, and shockingly sexy.

Especially for a *married couple!*

She could barely believe it was finally true. Ten years had been a long time to wait, but with the joy that now bound both their hearts, the past and the present melded together into the sweet, endless promise of the future. There was nothing but good luck ahead for them now, she knew.

The curse on the diamond was broken, but Drake's spell on her would last forever.

The spell was love.

THE EDITORS' CORNER

Hey! Look out your window. What do you see? Summer's finally in full bloom! And what does that mean? It means you can grab your four new LOVE-SWEPTs and head outdoors to read them! So when you're at the beach, in the backyard, or sitting on the dock of the bay, take care not to get sunburned while you bask in the warm summer sun reading your LOVESWEPTs!

Remember Georgia DeWitt, the woman who was jilted at the altar in DADDY MATERIAL? Well, she's back in **GEORGIA ON HIS MIND**, LOVE-SWEPT #842, Marcia Evanick's second chapter of her White Lace & Promises trilogy. Carpenter Levi Horst knows he has no business fantasizing about a woman who's clearly out of his league, especially when she's his boss! Georgia knows she doesn't inspire men to move mountains—her last experience taught her that. But when she sets up her own antiques business and discovers a kindred spirit who shares her secret dreams, she's forced to reconsider. Now all she has to do is convince Levi that they really aren't from two different worlds after all. In a story sparkling with wit and tender sensuality, Marcia tells us what can happen when two unlikely lovers are astonished by their heart's desires and decide to risk it all to become a family.

In **TRUST ME ON THIS**, LOVESWEPT #843 from award-winning Jennifer Crusie, con-buster Alec Prentice and reporter Dennie Banks are thrown together by a whim of fate, but both have their own agendas in mind. After Alec is convinced that Dennie is not in cahoots with a notorious con man, he enlists her help in trapping his quarry. Dennie wants to interview a woman for a story that's guaranteed to earn her the promotion she so richly deserves—and she'll do anything to get it. After offending the woman she was supposed to interview, Dennie thinks it's time for plan B. Enter Alec, who has promised to help if she'll agree to his terms. Can these two passionate partners in crime get their man *and* each other? (Of course they can, it's a LOVESWEPT!) But *how* they do it is another thing. Find out how in Jennifer Crusie's hilarious and fast-paced gem of a love story!

Got a fire extinguisher? Looks like Jack Riley and Mary Jo Simpson are gonna need it when they meet in a classic case of **SPONTANEOUS COMBUSTION**, LOVESWEPT #844. Mary Jo seems to need a hero, but even after Jack has fought through fire to rescue her, he still insists he's no hero. She trembles at his touch, a touch that thrills her no end. But it scares her even more. She's lost every man she's ever loved to the line of duty and fears this man will be no different. When she becomes Jack's prime suspect in an arson investigation, Jack must decide if trusting his mystery lady could mean getting burned. LOVE-SWEPT favorite Janis Reams Hudson returns in a steamy saga of a man and a woman torn between their desire to do what's right and their desire for each other.

Nicole Sanders would rather get stuck in the mud than jump into the car with sexy stranger Alex Coleman in **TELL ME NO LIES,** LOVESWEPT #845 by rising star Jill Shalvis. Alone for most of her life, Nicole is bewildered to learn that she's been purposely denied the one thing she wants most—family. Now she has to wade through a sea of lies that will ultimately force her to make the hardest decision of her life. Alex has always been a sucker for a damsel in distress, and Nicole is no exception. As he fights the walls around her soul, the key to her identity may be all that stands between a future of love and a past full of sorrow and bitterness. In a powerful story of longing and belonging, Jill Shalvis entangles a woman desperate for love with a man who promises to be all the family she'll ever need.

Happy reading!

With warmest wishes,

Shauna Summers   *Joy Abella*

Shauna Summers   Joy Abella
Editor   Administrative Editor

P.S. Look for these Bantam women's fiction titles coming in July. From *New York Times* bestselling author Nora Roberts comes a hardcover edition of **PUBLIC SECRETS**, a tale of a pop-music superstar's daughter who grows to womanhood amid secrets too painful to remember, too dangerous to forget. From Teresa Medeiros comes **TOUCH OF ENCHANTMENT**, the sequel to her national bestseller, BREATH OF MAGIC. The only thing Tabitha Lenox hates more than being a witch is being a rich witch. But when she finds a mysterious family heirloom, she is whisked back to an era of dragons, knights, magic—and love. Newcomer Annette Reynolds delivers **REMEMBER THE TIME**, a spellbinding romance full of emotion and passion, in the tradition of Fern Michaels. When Kate Armstrong's husband dies in a tragic accident, little does she know she will learn more about him in death than she ever did while he was alive. Can Kate overcome her grief to rediscover her true self and find the love and fulfillment she deserves?

For current information on Bantam's women's fiction, visit our new web site, ISN'T IT ROMANTIC, at the following address:

http://www.bdd.com/romance

Don't miss these extraordinary books by
your favorite Bantam authors

On sale in May

AFFAIR
by Amanda Quick

TWICE A HERO
by Susan Krinard

TEXAS WILDCAT
by Adrienne deWolfe

SWEET REVENGE
by Nora Roberts

AFFAIR

by
New York Times bestselling author

Amanda Quick

available in hardcover

*Charlotte Arkendale thinks she knows all there is
to know about men. But nothing in her
experience has prepared her for Baxter St. Ives. A
dedicated man of science, St. Ives finds himself
reluctantly embroiled in a murder investigation—
and at the mercy of a fierce and highly illogical
passion for Charlotte. Caught up in their web of
passion, the lovers are unaware that a killer stalks
them, plotting to separate them . . . or to see
them joined together forever—in death.*

"You leave me no option but to be blunt, Mr. St. Ives.
Unfortunately, the truth of the matter is that you are not
quite what I had in mind in the way of a man-of-affairs."
Charlotte Arkendale clasped her hands together on top
of the wide mahogany desk and regarded Baxter with a
critical eye. "I am sorry for the waste of your time."

The interview was not going well. Baxter adjusted the
gold-framed eyeglasses on the bridge of his nose and
silently vowed that he would not give in to the impulse
to grind his back teeth.

"Forgive me, Miss Arkendale, but I was under the impression that you wished to employ a person who appeared completely innocuous and uninteresting."

"Quite true."

"I believe your exact description of the ideal candidate
for the position was, and I quote, *a person who is as bland
as a potato pudding.*"

Charlotte blinked wide, disconcertingly intelligent, green eyes. "You do not comprehend me properly, sir."

"I rarely make mistakes, Miss Arkendale. I am nothing if not precise, methodical, and deliberate in my ways. Mistakes are made by those who are impulsive or inclined toward excessive passions. I assure you, I am not of that temperament."

"I could not agree with you more on the risks of a passionate nature," she said quickly. "Indeed, that is one of the problems—"

"Allow me to read to you precisely what you wrote in your letter to your recently retired man-of-affairs."

"There is no need. I am perfectly aware of what I wrote to Mr. Marcle."

Baxter ignored her. He reached into the inside pocket of his slightly rumpled coat and removed the letter he had stored there. He had read the damn thing so many times that he almost had it memorized, but he made a show of glancing down at the flamboyant handwriting.

" 'As you know, Mr. Marcle, I require a man-of-affairs to take your place. He must be a person who presents an ordinary, unassuming appearance. I want a man who can go about his business unnoticed; a gentleman with whom I can meet frequently without attracting undue attention or comment.

" 'In addition to the customary duties of a man-of-affairs, duties which you have fulfilled so very admirably during the past five years, sir, I must ask that the gentleman whom you recommend possess certain other skills.

" 'I shall not trouble you with the details of the situation in which I find myself. Suffice it to say that due to recent events I am in need of a stout, keenly alert individual who can be depended upon to protect my person. In short, I wish to employ a bodyguard as well as a man-of-affairs.

"'Expense, as always, must be a consideration. Therefore, rather than undertake the cost of engaging two men to fill two posts, I have concluded that it will prove more economical to employ one man who can carry out the responsibilities of both positions—'"

"Yes, yes, I recall my own words quite clearly," Charlotte interrupted testily. "But that is not the point."
Baxter doggedly continued:

"'I therefore request that you send me a respectable gentleman who meets the above requirements and who presents an appearance that is as bland as a potato pudding.'"

"I fail to see why you must repeat aloud everything on the page, Mr. St. Ives."
Baxter pressed on:

"'He must be endowed with a high degree of intelligence as I shall require him to make the usual delicate inquiries for me. But in his capacity as a bodyguard, he must also be skilled in the use of a pistol in case events take a nasty turn. Above all, Mr. Marcle, as you well know, he must be discreet.'"

"Enough, Mr. St. Ives." Charlotte picked up a small volume bound in red leather and slapped it smartly against the desktop to get his attention.
Baxter glanced up from the letter. "I believe I meet most of your requirements, Miss Arkendale."
"I am certain that you do meet a few of them." She favored him with a frosty smile. "Mr. Marcle would never have recommended you to me if that were not the

case. Unfortunately there is one very important qualification which you lack."

Baxter deliberately refolded the letter and slipped it back inside his coat. "You insisted upon a man who would draw little attention. A staid, unremarkable man-of-affairs."

"Yes, but—"

"Allow me to tell you that I am often described in those very terms. Bland as a potato pudding in every way."

Charlotte scowled. "Do not feed me that banbury tale. You most certainly are not a potato pudding. Just the opposite, in fact."

He stared at her. "I beg your pardon?"

She groaned. "You must know very well, sir, that your spectacles are a poor disguise."

"Disguise?" He wondered if he had got the wrong address and the wrong Charlotte Arkendale. Perhaps he had got the wrong town. "What in the name of the devil do you believe me to be concealing?"

"Surely you are not suffering from the illusion that those spectacles mask your true nature."

"My true nature?" Baxter lost his grip on his patience. "Bloody hell, just what am I, if not innocuous and un-prepossessing?"

She spread her hands wide. "You have the look of a man of strong passions who has mastered his temperament with even stronger powers of self-mastery."

"I beg your pardon?"

Her eyes narrowed with grim determination. "Such a man cannot hope to go about unnoticed. You are bound to attract attention when you conduct business on my behalf. I cannot have that in my man-of-affairs. I require someone who can disappear into a crowd. Someone whose face no one recalls very clearly. Don't you understand, sir? You give the appearance of being rather, well, to be quite blunt, *dangerous*."

The nationally bestselling author of *Prince of Shadows*
and *Star-Crossed* weaves a thrilling new tale of time
travel, intrigue, and romantic adventure.

TWICE A HERO

by Susan Krinard

*MacKenzie "Mac" Sinclair is cursed. So is the
whole Sinclair family. Ever since her great-great-
grandfather Peregrine returned from an
expedition to the Mayan ruins with half of a
mysterious pendant—and without his partner,
Liam O'Shea—they've been haunted by
misfortune. That's why Mac's beloved grandfather
wants her to undertake a solo expedition . . . to
return the pendant to the ruins of Tikal and find
a way to atone for whatever part Peregrine
played in Liam's disappearance. But when Mac
braves the steamy, primitive jungle, something
extraordinary happens: she blunders into the arms
of an eerily familiar explorer. Now she's in for
more adventure than she bargained for. Because
she's found Liam O'Shea . . . alive, well, and
seductively real. In the year 1884.*

The woman was obviously an actress of considerable
talent. Or she was quite mad.

"1884?" she repeated, her low voice hoarse. "Did you
say—*1884*? But that's not possible."

Liam regarded her stunned expression with suspicious
bemusement. Simple insanity did fit hand in glove with
the rest of her: thin, wiry, distinctly peculiar with her cap
of short hair and bold dark eyes, sharp-tongued, dressed
top to toe in men's clothing of an odd cut, and carrying a
newfangled electric lantern the likes of which he had

never seen in all his travels. And alone here in the jungle, first claiming she'd been with a full party of explorers and then insisting that no man had brought her.

And then there were her odd manner of speech, her absurd assertions of hotels in the jungle and omnibuses from Flores, her reaction to Tikal—as if she'd expected to see something entirely different, though she claimed to know the ruins.

Yes, one could almost believe she was in a state of mental disturbance—if not for the photograph she had so carelessly allowed him to see. The one taken here in these very ruins four years ago.

"What did you expect, Miss MacKenzie?" he asked. "Maybe you've been in the jungle too long after all."

Her dark brows drew down, and her gaze grew unfocused. "Okay, Mac," she muttered. "Time to wake up. This isn't happening."

Was this act a way of protecting herself, avoiding his questions because she'd revealed too much? Liam couldn't forget the shock he'd felt when he'd seen her with the photograph. Until that moment she'd been only an unforeseen burden to dispose of in the nearest safe place, some eccentric suffragist amateur explorer who'd been lost or deliberately abandoned, left for him to save.

After what had happened yesterday, he'd never considered doing otherwise.

The sharp sting of recent memory made the bitterness rise in his throat: Perry's revelation, the knowledge that Liam's trust in his partner had been entirely misplaced, the fight, drinking to drown the rage and loss, waking up this morning to find the bearers, mules, and nearly all the supplies, gone. With Perry.

Abandoned. Betrayed by the one man he'd thought he could trust. The man who stood beside him in that damned photograph.

He'd thought the girl in far more desperate straits than himself. She was of the weaker sex, in spite of her ridiculous beliefs to the contrary. But now—now he felt a grinding suspicion in his gut, wild thoughts fully as mad as the woman's incoherent ramblings and disjointed explanations.

Liam scowled at Miss MacKenzie's inward stare. She wasn't the only one with wits gone begging. A woman? Even Perry wouldn't sink so far. And there hadn't been time. But after yesterday nothing seemed beyond possibility.

And their meeting had seemed more than merely coincidence.

He studied her, chin on fist, allowing himself full rein to his imagination. Perry would never assume that his erstwhile partner would be distracted by a woman like this. She was hardly beautiful. Her hair was ridiculously short, her brows too heavy, her stubborn jaw too strong, her figure too narrow. Though she'd proven she was, in fact, female enough when the rain had soaked through her shirt.

He found himself gazing at her chest. More there than he'd first noticed; come to think of it, she couldn't pass for a boy, not unless that loose shirt were completely dry. . . .

You've been without a woman too long, O'Shea. He snorted. *No.* At best Perry would expect him to be delayed further, getting the girl back to civilization. That would neatly fit in with his intentions.

Liam's fist slammed into the wet stone of the temple. Perry knew too damned much about him. He knew Liam wouldn't leave any woman alone in the jungle, no matter what his circumstances—without supplies or bearers or even a single scrawny mule. . . .

Because you trusted him. The rage bubbled up again, and with very little effort he could imagine his fist connecting with Perry's superior, aristocratic face.

By the saints, it wasn't over yet. When Liam got back to San Francisco—

"That's it."

He snapped out of his grim reverie. Miss MacKenzie—"Mac," the name she had called herself and which suited her so well—had apparently recovered her senses. Or ended her game. She was on her feet, looking out over the jungle with set jaw and a lunatic's obsession.

"I'm going back," she announced.

Liam rose casually. The top of her cropped head came almost to his chin; tall for a woman. He hadn't realized that before.

"Back where—'Mac'?" he drawled.

Her stare was no longer unfocused. She looked at him as if she'd like to pitch him over the side of the pyramid. "Only my friends call me Mac," she said, "and you're sure as hell not my friend. You're a figment of my overheated imagination."

He gave a startled bark of laughter. Whoever and whatever she was, she had the ridiculous ability to make him hover between laughter and outrage. No woman had ever managed that before. She was too damned good at keeping him off balance. Was that her purpose—and Perry's?

To hell with that. If there was anything to his suspicions, he'd learn soon enough.

"So," he said, "you don't think I'm real?" He took one long step, closing the gap between them, and felt her shudder as his chest brushed hers. He could feel the little tips of her breasts, hardening through the shirt. He felt an unexpected hardening in his own body. "What proof do you need, eh?"

She tried to step back, but the temple wall was behind her. "You . . . uh . . ." She thrust out her jaw and glared. "Let me by. I'm going back to the ruins."

"If I'm not real, Mac, you should have no difficulty walking through me."

Suddenly she chuckled. The sound had a hysterical edge. "Great idea," she said. With the full force of her slender weight she pushed against him. The assault drove him back a pace. She stepped to the side, strode to the rim of the temple platform, and slid her foot over the edge.

He caught her arm just as an ancient stone step gave way under her foot. "Are you so eager to break your neck?" he snapped. "Or are you more afraid of something else?"

Her eyes were wide and dark and surprisingly large, rimmed with thick lashes he hadn't noticed before. There was a slight trembling to the lids and at the corners of her lips, as if she'd realized how easy it would have been to tumble down that steep incline in her reckless attempt to escape.

Escape *him*. Was that what she was trying to do?

From the delightful, passionate voice of

Adrienne deWolfe

author of *Texas Outlaw* and *Texas Lover*
comes

TEXAS WILDCAT

*Bailey McShane has had a crush on Zack Rawlins
since she was thirteen and he was courting her
cousin. Now, nearly ten years later, she and Zack
hardly seem able to exchange a civil word with
each other. Bailey knows that is partly due to a
severe drought in Texas, which has been setting
sheepherders—like herself—against cattle
ranchers—like Zack. But Bailey is sure she and
Zack can at least be friends; so when he comes to
her ranch one day with a peace offering, she
gladly invites him to stay for dinner—a dinner
that ends with them both drinking too much
moonshine as a storm gathers overhead. . . .*

"Rain," Bailey whispered.

She jumped to her feet and ran a bit unsteadily to the
window, planting her hands on the sill and sticking her
head and shoulders outside. When she turned her face
to the skies, wind kicked up her sheaf of hair, and thun-
der crashed like two colliding locomotives, shaking the
wooden frame around her. She giggled like a child.

"Rain!" she shouted, turning to face Zack, her cheeks
streaked by the droplets that were sliding into her collar.
"Let's go watch!"

Before he could draw breath enough to answer, she
grabbed the room's lone lamp and raced into the pitch
blackness of the hallway.

Thrown into darkness, Zack muttered an oath, not waiting for his eyes to grow accustomed before he pushed back his chair. The moonshine hit him full force then, and his knees wobbled. The very idea that some slip of a sheepherder was holding her liquor better than he was was enough to make the blood rush to his head. He grabbed his hat and fanned his face.

"C'mon, Zack!"

Her voice floated in to him above the banging of the front door, and he grinned. He couldn't help it. Rain, by God. There was actually rain!

Draping his Stetson haphazardly over his brow, he hurried across the unfamiliar floor, banging his shin on the doorstop and stubbing his toe on a sitting-room chair. He hardly noticed, though. He was too eager to follow that beckoning light to the circle of brightness it cast on the parched and withered yard. Bailey had balanced the lamp on the porch railing, and when he pushed open the bottom half of the door, he spied her dancing in its yellow blaze. Laughing, she spun like a top, her arms outstretched, her face turned to the heavens. He stumbled to a halt, simply staring.

Her exuberance had loosed her hair from its leather thong, and it whipped around her like slick amber tongues, twining around her upper arms, slapping her buttocks, caressing her thighs. The rain had plastered her jeans to her skin, and the white cotton of her shirt was growing nigh transparent. He swallowed hard, unable to do the gentlemanly thing, unable to tear his gaze away from that sheer clinging fabric and the feminine peaks and valleys it outlined so faithfully.

She crooked her forefinger at him in a beckoning gesture. "C'mere, cowboy," she said huskily.

"What for?" he drawled, stepping off the porch.

"So I can do . . . *this*!"

Before he could guess her intention, she snatched the Stetson from his head and dashed away, whooping like an Indian in a rain dance.

"Hey!" He couldn't stop himself from laughing. "Give me back my hat, woman!"

"Not unless you catch me first!"

"I'll catch you, all right," he growled, and charged after her.

Her heels clattered on the planks of the bridge. In a flash of lightning, he saw her balanced precariously on the bridge's railless edge. He was just about to rush to her when he heard her gasp. Suddenly she wobbled. Her arms and legs flailed. In the next instant she was toppling, shrieking at the top of her lungs.

"Bailey!"

Without thought for his boots or spurs, Zack ran for the stream bank. Slipping and sliding, he scrambled through the rain-slickened reeds and plunged into the water. All he could think in that terrible, mind-numbing moment was that he'd lost her. He'd lost his precious Bailey.

Then he heard a splash.

It was followed by a giggle.

A shadow rose before him, slipping water in cascades, dumping another hatful over itself when it crammed the Stetson onto its head.

"That was fun!" the shadow shouted cheerfully.

Well, that was it. The final straw. Zack grabbed her arm, which threw them both off balance, and they landed side by side in about two feet of water. With a feral sound that was half frustration and half mirth, he fastened his lips over hers, drawing her tongue deep into his mouth. With a hunger he hadn't realized he possessed, he tasted and feasted, plundering the hot, wet mystery behind her breaths. His craving grew more insistent, more demanding with each intoxicating moment.

"Bailey," he groaned, struggling to remember his code of honor, struggling to beat back the desire that crackled along his electrified nerves. "We have to . . . You need to . . . It's time you dried off."

He boosted her to her feet, then hoisted her into his arms.

"Where are you taking me?" she asked, sounding childlike and uncertain as he waded toward the reeds.

"Inside, out of the rain."

"What for?"

"So you can change your wet clothes."

She seemed to think about that for a moment, worrying her bottom lip. Then she loosed a dreamy sigh and dropped her head against his shoulder. "Good. I always wanted you to be the one, Zack. . . ."

From the *New York Times* bestselling
author of **Montana Sky**

NORA ROBERTS

creates a classic suspense tale of a father's
betrayal and a daughter's quest for

SWEET REVENGE

Now available in paperback

The child of a fabled Hollywood star and a charming, titled playboy, Princess Adrianne lives a life most people would envy. But her pampered-rich-girl pose is a ruse . . . a carefully calculated effort to hide a dangerous truth. For ten years, Adrianne has lived for revenge. As a child, she could only watch the cruelty hidden behind the facade of her parents' fairy-tale marriage. Now, though nothing will bring her mother back, Adrianne is ready to make her father pay. As the infamous jewel thief, The Shadow, Adrianne is poised to steal the Sun and Moon—a necklace beyond price—and to taste the sweetness of her long-sought revenge . . . until she meets a man who seems to divine her every secret—and has his own private reasons for getting close to Princess Adrianne.

On sale in June

TOUCH OF ENCHANTMENT
by Teresa Medeiros

REMEMBER THE TIME
by Annette Reynolds

PUBLIC SECRETS
by Nora Roberts